THE CLEANER

A DARK BRATVA ROMANCE

RENEE ROSE

RENEE ROSE ROMANCE

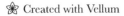 Created with Vellum

WANT FREE RENEE ROSE BOOKS?

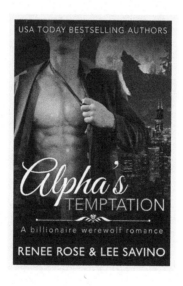

Go to http://subscribepage.com/alphastemp to sign up for Renee Rose's newsletter and receive a free copy of *Alpha's Temptation, Theirs to Protect, Owned by the Marine* and more. In addition to the free stories, you will also get bonus epilogues, special pricing, exclusive previews and news of new releases.

Adrian

    Come on out, dietka. I'm waiting.

I prop a shoulder against a brick wall, watching the entrance to the flat across the street where my mark, Kateryna Poval, lives. The incessant Liverpool rain has paused for the moment, but fog nestles close to the sidewalks, occasionally obscuring my view.

A girl who fits her description emerges from the flat, but it can't be her. This one appears too young. Her long dark hair is in two braids, and she's wearing a school uniform: knee-high socks with a short, pleated skirt and white blouse…

Huh. Hold up. Maybe she's not as young as I thought.

The blouse is tied up under her breasts to bare her flat belly, and the throat is open *way* too low for a school uniform, giving view to a rather impressive rack. And she's not wearing a jacket or necktie. Plus the skirt is far too short.

Besides, it's ten at night.

So that's not a student in a uniform, it's my mark in

some kind of costume. She has a tiny backpack strapped to her back to complete the schoolgirl look although it's more purse-sized than anything that would hold books or folders.

Why isn't she wearing a fucking jacket? It's not frigid like Chicago or Russia, but England is still cold in January, for Christ's sake. I don't know why I give a fuck, but it bothers me.

I stay in the shadows, following the young woman on the opposite side of the street.

It was nearly impossible to get any photos of Kateryna—she has zero social media presence, which is unheard of for a young woman of twenty—but our hacker got into her secondary school records to retrieve an older photo.

Leon Poval's daughter went to a private prep school where she was enrolled under the last name Kovalenko, but she completed her secondary studies two years ago. Now she attends a small art school here, which seems strange. Surely, they have those back in Ukraine. Maybe Poval thinks she's safer hidden here.

I don't give a fuck, so long as she has a pulse and can be used as leverage against him.

I trail her to the bus stop where she perches on the backrest of a cement bench, her feet—which are in platform heels—on the seat. She flicks one of her dark braids off her shoulder and blows a bubble with her gum. I can't quite figure out if she really is an insolent overgrown teen or if she has some kind of school-girl fetish. I think there's a Japanese fashion trend that is sexy school uniforms—maybe that's her jam. Or could she be a stripper? I seem to recall Pavel telling me the school-girl thing was a popular stripper outfit. Or was it in the BDSM dungeons he went to? Fuck if I know. I don't go out much. Not with my sister's fragile state.

I pull out my phone and study the photo Dima sent me, comparing it to the young woman at the bus stop.

The girl in the photo is a perfect match. She's a few years younger in the picture, wearing a more conservative uniform with the jacket and necktie, and she appears as innocent and young as this version seems saucy.

The bus approaches, and I cross the street, hanging back until she boards, then climbing on and sliding into a seat in the front. I pull the knit cap I'm wearing down low over my forehead. She's behind me, but I can watch her reflection in the windshield.

She wears a slender gold hoop nose ring, and she puts earbuds in her ears and scrolls through something on her phone. She hasn't noticed me, which is good because I don't plan on grabbing her tonight.

The cargo ship I've arranged to transport her to the U.S. won't dock for a few days. I'm just keeping an eye on her for now. It's probably not my smartest move, since I have no practice in subtlety when it comes to stalking. I don't want to alert her to my presence. But I also don't want to lose her. I've been looking for her father for over a year now. Ever since he gave me the slip after I burned down his sex slave den masquerading as a sofa factory.

When Dima, my bratva brother and Russia's finest hacker, told me he discovered Poval had a daughter, I had to seize my chance.

I won't hurt her. Not like Poval hurt Nadia.

But I sure as hell will make him think I have. I want him to suffer, believing I'm going to enact every last indignity and trauma he inflicted on my sister.

The bus stops a few times, and Kateryna hops off. I wait a few beats until the doors close then surge toward the front door, making the bus driver curse and throw the door open again.

I slip out without her seeing me and follow at a distance. She's in a sketchy, industrial part of town, but there are cars parked everywhere. Something is definitely happening. A warehouse party. Or maybe they still do raves in Liverpool. Either way, I'm going to have to go in if I don't want to lose track of her. It looks like the place is packed.

I watch her knock on the door. When it swings open, music blares from the place and a big guy who appears to be some kind of bouncer lets her in. I wait sixty seconds then follow.

"Password?" the door guy demands.

I pull a fifty pound note out of my pocket and tuck it in the guy's palm. "Appreciate it," I say, wishing my Russian accent wasn't so damn strong. At least the tattoos on my knuckles don't work against me with a guy like this.

He gives me a once over. "You gotta friend in here?"

Fuck.

"Yeah," I say, my brain scrambling. "I'm friends with Kateryna. Ukrainian girl? Rocks a schoolgirl outfit?" Maybe if I'm lucky, this guy will think my accent is Ukrainian, too.

It works. He pushes the door open. "Kat just got here." He jerks his head inside.

I hope giving her name doesn't come back to bite me in the ass. I would've been better off making something else up. Oh well, too late now.

I enter the darkened warehouse. It's lit with colored lights like a nightclub and music blasts from big speakers. There's a DJ playing in the corner, and nice lounge furniture around the edges of the room. The place is packed with bodies bouncing and undulating to the beat. It's definitely a rave. Kateryna–or I guess it's Kat here–is nowhere to be seen, but she fits right in with the other scantily-clad girls.

The good news is that I can blend in. The bad news is that I have no idea where my mark has disappeared to. I shove my hands in the pockets of my jacket and make my way casually through the crowd, bobbing my head to the music like I'm just here for the beats.

Turns out, it's not hard to find Kateryna at all because she climbed on top of a large wooden crate and is swaying her hips in half-time to the music, inviting every *mudak* below her to look up that short fucking skirt of hers.

Which isn't my problem, obviously. Still, my fingers close into fists in my pockets thinking about the bad things that could happen to her here. She came alone—which is pretty fucking strange. Girls always run in packs. And now she's inviting all kinds of male attention.

Oh shit. I look away when we make brief eye contact. Stepping back, I move along the wall and pull out my phone, pretending to text someone.

"Hi." A female voice pulls my attention at the same time the speaker tugs my sleeve.

You've gotta be fucking kidding me.

I've been made.

Kat stands in front of me, a wide, saucy smile showing off the straightest, whitest set of teeth I've ever seen. She looks up at me from under a curtain of dark bangs, and I discover her eyes are a surprising shade of electric blue. She's not wearing any color on her lids, but the thick black eyeliner that extends beyond the outer corners of her eyes only accentuates the light color of her irises.

I don't answer her because…fuck. I shouldn't have let her see me to begin with. I might be a decent cleaner, but I'm a piss-poor tail.

She's still holding my sleeve, and she slides her hand

down to close her fingers around my fist. "Nice tattoos. That's Russian, right?" She pulls my knuckles closer to her face to examine the Cyrillic letters that are an acronym for my bratva cell. Her hands are small, her touch soft.

I pull my hand back and scowl, trying to get her to leave. Although I guess it's too late. She's seen me. She won't forget my face now. *"Da."*

Her smile grows wider. "I'm Ukrainian. My name is Kat." She holds her palm out for me to shake. When I don't take it, she grips mine and gives it a single pump.

Bozhe moi, this girl has terrible instincts. Can she not tell that I'm trouble? I'm literally here to ruin her life. I wear a permanent scowl. I don't look like a nice guy. I wasn't particularly friendly even before her father destroyed my sister, and now? I'm fucking lethal. She's touching the tattoos that prove it.

Poor judgment must be why her father sequestered her away in England. Even so, it's a wonder she hasn't been torn apart yet.

I force myself to pretend I belong here. I'm just another party-goer. I arch a brow and scan her outfit. "You old enough to be here?"

She snaps her gum at me. "What do you think?"

"I think you should go home before your daddy finds out you snuck out the window on a school night."

Her smile dims. I'm not sure if it's the mention of her father or my continuing assholery. She flips me the middle finger and finally leaves, her skirt swishing up when she turns, giving me a flash of chaste white cotton granny-panties.

What. The fuck?

I watch her departing back trying to figure out what just happened. Kateryna Poval is nothing like I expected. I thought she'd be spoiled, certainly. Possibly sheltered and naive. I guess I braced myself in case she was fragile and sweet. A delicate flower I would crush and sully to get back at her father.

Well, *pretend* to crush and sully. I'm not a monster like Poval. I don't defile and destroy young girls for profit or pleasure.

I didn't expect an over-sexualized wild-child running around Liverpool begging for trouble. But maybe this is what spoiled crime princess looks like on her.

I guess it makes my job easier. I wasn't sure I'd have the stomach for frightening an innocent girl. This one doesn't seem to know when to be scared, and she certainly doesn't seem innocent.

Kateryna Poval is trouble waiting to happen.

And I'm the guy who's going to bring it crashing down on her.

Kat

That guy was an asshole. A hot asshole, but still. Why am I always drawn to the jerks?

Oh yeah: daddy issues.

That's what Delaney, my psychotherapist, seems to think anyway. She said I will continue to act out, rebel, and seek attention from the wrong kind of men until I'm willing to work on healing the wounds my father inflicted.

But working on anything related to my father will happen when Hell freezes over.

Also, maybe I want to act out, rebel, and seek attention from the wrong kind of men. I secretly desire being taken in hand and punished. I sort of feel like she was kink-shaming me.

Hating the way that guy made me feel off-kilter, I

picture myself as a lump of clay on the wheel and find my exact center as I head to the bathrooms at the back of the warehouse. There's a long queue, so I take my place with the crowd of other girls.

"Hey, girl," Shellee, a frequent party-goer says as she comes out of the stall, grabbing my arm. She's already rolling on ecstasy; her pupils are almost as big as her irises. She's fully in love with me in this moment because she's fully in love with everything right now. "Do you have a tampon?"

"I sure do." I whirl my backpack purse off one shoulder to dig in and grab the tampon, which I hand to her.

She closes her fingers around it and my hand and strokes my cheek with her free hand. "Thank you *so* much," she gushes. "I love you. I'm so glad you're here. You're amazing, do you know that?"

We're not actually friends. Just acquaintances. I honestly don't have real friends. I'm too *extra* for most of them. Too popular with the boys. Too sexual. Too rich, even for the girls at the prep school. Plus, I'm different. I'm not English. My father's businesses aren't legit. I learned the day I arrived in Liverpool that I didn't fit in and should stop trying.

Delaney says that's why I seek out intense sexual experiences–I'm filing a void created by my lack of meaningful friendships.

I think I'm just kinky. Is that so wrong?

"So are you," I tell Shellee. "Here, cut in line with me, so you can get back in there." I tug her in front of me.

She turns around and starts petting me again, fingering a braid as she smiles dreamily in my direction.

"You're having a good time?"

"*So* much fun." She squints her gaze at me. "Are you rolling?"

"Nope. I can't. I have a history test tomorrow."

"Oh my God!" Her eyes widen in exaggerated surprise. "Why are you here?" She tugs my braid. "Just kidding." Her playful shove makes me stumble in my platform heels. "I'm glad you're here. I'm always glad when I see you. You're the best."

I'm not even sure if she knows my name, but it's okay. I have no illusions about what this scene is. It's not where you go to make lasting meaningful relationships. Which is why I happen to love it.

I came to reward myself for studying all day for my exam. My father's stipulation for me staying in England for college was that I maintain 7s–the UK equivalent of straight A's. Considering I got 4's and a few 3's in high school, it's a bit of an up-level. But there's no freaking way I'm going home.

Especially not when I finally found something I like.

I mean, beyond rave parties and kinky sex, which Delaney says are extensions of my Daddy issues.

My last term in secondary school, we got a new art teacher, Ms. Banff. She got the school to buy a wheel and taught us pottery. I suppose it was another way to flip my dad the bird–show him I'm the useless, brainless, waste of space he apparently thinks I am–but I decided to become a potter. I totally fell in love with it.

I like the feel of the clay in my hands. The spin of the wheel. The way a bowl takes shape and collapses with the touch of a finger. So now I would do anything to stay in England and keep studying art. I crave the pottery wheel as much as I crave these dance parties. Or a big, muscled guy who scowls and never shows you that he likes you.

It's finally my turn to use the toilet, and when I get out,

Shellee has already disappeared. Which is fine, since I didn't come here to see her anyway.

I'm not sure why I came, actually. It's more of an addiction than anything else. I crave the sensuality of the place. I like to dress up and feel sexy and maybe hook up with a hot guy. Preferably one who's into a little kink. I love a big rough guy who will hold me down and choke me. Or spank me. Or tie me up. I'm a little maso at heart, and the endorphin release and thrill I get from acting out my fantasies is what I need to get through the week.

Let's be honest, though. That big, rough guy doesn't actually exist. Or when he does, he comes with a slice of danger I really shouldn't tempt.

Yet tempt it I do.

I make my way out of the bathroom. The warehouse is packed with people now. Probably more than a legit club would allow for fire code. I soak up the energy like a drug. Looking for trouble, I climb on top of a platform to dance again. I bounce and swirl to the music, scanning the crowd. I spot the Russian up against a wall watching me. He has dark hair, brown eyes and wears what looks like a permanent scowl.

Why would he be such a dick if he's interested? I could've sworn he was interested before, which was why I went over to him. He has the right vibe. Definitely my type. Surly. Rough. Tattoos that probably mean he's done bad things. His shoulders are broad. It's hard to tell under his leather jacket, but they look well-muscled. I bet he could dish out a spanking that would make me cream my panties. I totally pegged him as a sadist.

Guess I was wrong.

It's not like I'm really good at picking the right ones. I've had a half-dozen fails in the last three months alone.

I keep my gaze on my Russian while I dance, but he

looks away with a scowl. I know he feels my gaze. I swear he's looking away on purpose. What is it about *hard to get* that just makes a girl want to try more? I check my tits–the double D's I had by age twelve. They are perfectly displayed by my blouse. I definitely look hot. No reason for him not to respond. Unless he's here for someone else. But why does he keep looking at me?

There. He looked again.

I turn to give him a view of my ass as I take a slow swivel to the floor and back up again.

"Kat!" A guy calls me from the floor below.

Oh great. David, one of my past mistakes. I blow him a kiss but keep dancing.

He grabs my ankle, forcing me to stop dancing or lose my balance. Yeah, this was why he was a mistake. I mistook his disrespectful vibe for dominance. Truth is, he's more of a bully.

"Come here!" He reaches for me.

"No, I'm good," I say. Just because we hooked up once doesn't mean I'm your go-to, buddy.

He flashes a tiny Ziploc baggie at me. "Wanna roll?"

I shake my head again. "No thanks. I have a test tomorrow." He wins no points with me for offering free drugs. I'm not fooling around again with him even if I'm not sober. He was sloppy and only in it for himself. *Yech.*

He shrugs and moves on, and I continue to dance. I'm joined on the platform by a few other guys who dance closer and closer until one settles a hand on my waist and connects his hips to my ass to grind against me. I let him because it feels good. I came here for male attention, and I'm getting it. Another guy moves in from the front, so I'm sandwiched between them.

The guy from behind palms my left breast. He's not completely unskilled. He finds my nipple and pinches it through my blouse and push-up bra. I shove my ass back and let my head rest against his shoulder.

"I like your outfit," the first guy shouts over the music.

It's not a particularly stupid thing to say, but I sort of wish he'd just keep his mouth shut. I'm trying to have a fantasy moment here, and the inane comments pull me out. The guy behind me slides a hand down the front of my thigh and squeezes my leg muscles.

I've never had two guys at once, but the group-grope thing happens at these raves. Everyone's feeling the love, and they just want to pass it along. The problem is, it's usually a lot of groping and no finish. The ecstasy makes people too blissed out to have any motivation to get to climax. Another reason I skip the drugs, other than a CBD gummy now and then when I can't sleep. I'm looking for a different endorphin hit.

"How old are you?" the guy in front of me asks. He probably wants to make sure he won't end up in jail or something.

"Twenty." I don't feel twenty. I feel thirty because I've been away from home for so long. And also thirteen, the age I was when my dad shipped me off. He caught me making out with a boy and decided I needed to be sent off to an all-girls boarding school.

As if that would keep me out of trouble. It only cemented my desire to be bad.

Do you want to be bad, Kat, or are you actually craving someone to tell you you're good? That's what Delaney asked me last time we discussed me going to raves.

"I wouldn't mind being called *good girl* when I obey," I'd sassed back.

"Nice." The guy nods, his leer appreciative.

We dance for a while, but things don't escalate much. People lose focus when they're rolling.

"I'm going to take a break," I tell the guys after a while because I'm getting hot, bored, and thirsty.

They immediately jump down off the box and follow me to the makeshift bar where three kids in knit caps and earrings are selling energy drinks and water. I buy water, crack the bottle and turn to find my two admirers are still standing there like eager beavers.

Meh. I was kind of done with them, hoping for something a little more interesting. My gaze wanders, looking for the Russian again. I don't know why I'm so obsessed with him. I guess because he turned me down. Why do I always go for the one who will reject me?

The guys each take me by a hand, dragging me to a dark corner. I'm not on board, but I'm not totally ready to jump-ship either. I mean, I guess I'll see what they have to offer.

"What's this?" David cuts off our path with a giant smile in place. "This looks very fun."

Now I'm done.

"Yeah, I don't know." I try to shake loose from the two guys holding my hands.

"You need a little mood enhancer," David says, pulling out the baggie of pills again.

"Can I have one?" the guy to my right says.

"No. It's for her." David extracts the pill, and before I know it's coming, he pops it between my teeth.

"Hey!" I try to spit it out, but David laughs, clapping a hand over my mouth.

"Wait, wait, wait. Just swallow it, Kat. It will be fun."

I struggle, but the other guys don't help me out even though they're crowding into me from the sides, holding me in place for David to keep his hand over my mouth.

I'm pissed now, and–dammit–I already swallowed the stupid pill! These fuckers.

"Here, drink your water, Kat." David wraps his hand over mine on the water bottle and brings it to my mouth.

I'm still struggling just to get everyone's hands off me. As I flail, I hear a loud crack of bone on bone and then David falls. I stare at him sprawled out on the dirty concrete floor. Did I do that?

And then I understand. Because there are six feet of pissed-off Russian standing in front of us.

His lips peel back from his teeth in a snarl, and he glares at the two guys standing next to me. "Go."

They go. They disappear so fast you'd think there was a fire in the place.

I open my mouth, about to protest that I didn't really need the help when the Russian tosses me over his shoulder and clomps out of the warehouse.

2

Adrian

Crazy girl making bad fucking choices.

What was I supposed to do? Let three guys date rape her right there in the warehouse? *Bozhe moi*, there were hundreds of people there, and no one else saw what was happening? I'm the only guy who stepped in to stop that bullshit?

I seriously hate this world. My gender. All humans.

I don't know what those guys gave her, but Kat is already giggling, and she hasn't even kicked up a fuss about me carrying her out of there in such an undignified manner. Honestly, I'd be surprised if the drugs even kicked in yet. I think this is just her natural reaction. I'd put her down, but now I'm all in. I'll just have to move my timetable up and kidnap her tonight.

The cargo ship doesn't leave for two more days, which means I'll have to keep her in my rented cottage until we leave. It's not ideal. Not at all.

Maxim, our bratva's fixer, taught me to think through a situation for all possible angles. Anywhere you could get caught or leave a trail. The ship offers a great deal of safety. I arranged passage through the local bratva. No questions will be asked about the girl.

But keeping her prisoner here in the city?

A lot of things can go wrong.

"Okay, big man. You are very heroic. You can put me down now." I like her accent. Ukrainian plus English. It's very cute.

I ignore her, trying to think. How will I even get her on a bus against her will? Why in the fuck didn't I rent a car?

But then, how would I have followed her? No, I just have to slow down.

She's just been roofied or whatever they gave her. I might not have to take her against her will.

The idea of tricking her turns my stomach, but it seems like the best option. It's not like tricking her is any worse than putting a bag over her head and strong-arming her out of here.

She squeezes my butt. "Where are we going, big man?"

Big man. Very cute. I'm not that big. Not like Oleg, our bratva enforcer.

I drop her to her feet, and we stare at each other. I should think of something slick and suave to say, but I already fucked it up by throwing her over my shoulder. Besides, slick and suave aren't my things. I have to work hard just to make my English come out right.

She's pretty–heartbreakingly pretty. She reminds me a bit of Oleg's girlfriend Story. Classic beauty underneath the counter-culture getup.

"What in the *fuck* did you think you were doing?" I demand.

Nope, not slick or suave. That was the opposite of charming. *Blyad'.* I probably will have to throw her back over my shoulder and walk all the way back.

But she seems to like my outburst. She smiles and leans into me, her hands molding to my chest. "Sorry, Daddy," she says.

Excuse me?

My frown grows deeper. "What is fucking *wrong* with you?"

She laughs. "Take it easy, big man. I didn't need your rescue, as gallant as it was. I can handle myself with men."

White hot rage runs through me. Not toward her, but toward all the men on Earth because I know with total certainty, she can't handle them. Bad things happen to girls like her.

Horrible things. I live with the aftermath of what can happen every day.

"You have no idea!" I snap. "Do you even know what they gave you? Did you swallow it?"

"It was molly. It's fine. I've taken it before. Nothing bad will happen other than me feeling like crap tomorrow for my history test. You know, I might as well go enjoy it." She pushes back from me abruptly. "Don't worry, you don't need to take care of me. I'm going back."

I catch her arm, and she rubberbands back to me, bumping against my chest. She's almost a foot shorter than I am and soft in all the right places. I resist the urge to settle my hands on her waist like a lover. "No, you're not."

She grins like she loves me getting bossy. That's when it dawns on me. I admit I was slow, but it's coming together: the outfit. Calling me *Daddy*.

Kateryna is kinky as fuck. As kinky as my bratva brother Pavel and his slave girlfriend Kayla. She's into role play and cosplay and all that shit. I pivot with this new knowledge and think fast.

"You're going home," I tell her imperiously.

17

Yep. I was right. She loves it. She leans into me. "Are you taking me?" she purrs.

"*Da.* I'm fucking taking you." I shrug out of my leather jacket and drape it over her slender shoulders. Crazy girl coming out with no jacket in January. Although I can see why–it would've been hard to dance with it on, and there wasn't exactly a coat check at the door.

"Let's go before drugs kick in." I left out the article again. In my head, I hear Ravil, my Chicago Bratva boss, correcting me. *Before* the *drugs kick in.* I pull her along, heading for the bus stop.

She falls into step beside me, stealing a sidelong glance and hiding a smile. "Are you always this grumpy when you play hero?"

"I'm not the hero. I'm the villain, *dietka.*"

"What is *dietka*? I understand some Russian, but I don't know that word."

"It's like…*kid* or *babe.*"

"In a sweet way or a mean way?"

"What do you think?"

She looks over at me again. "Mean, probably," she grumbles. I think she's pouting.

It's obnoxious and annoying, and the fact that she's beautiful makes it damn cute. I'll bet it works with all the guys.

Good thing I'm not one of them. I pity any guy who drops into her big pot of hot mess crazy. She was one night away from disaster. The way I see it, I'll be doing her a favor by pulling her out of this existence.

I know I'm trying to justify what probably can't be justified. Kat is as innocent as Nadia. She doesn't deserve me using her as a pawn no matter how horrible her father is. But that can't be helped. She is the only lead I've had on the guy in over a year. She's my one ticket to evening the score for Nadia.

I don't have a clue about the bus schedule, but Kat leans against the bus stop sign like she expects one soon, so I fold my arms across my chest to wait with her.

"How did you know I took the bus?" she demands. She may be reckless, but she's not stupid.

Noted.

"I was on the same bus as you."

"You were?"

"*Da.*"

"What's your plan?" she asks.

I must be feeling guilty because for a moment I think she knows she's my prisoner. But no. She just means for tonight.

"I take you home. Put you to bed. End of story."

Or something like that. Take her home. Tie her up in her bed. Figure out what the fuck to do next.

"That means you're coming in?" She twirls a braid around her finger. "So you can put me to bed?"

"You have roommate? *A* roommate?" I correct my English.

"Nope." She pops her pink lips on the "p," drawing my attention to her mouth. Now that I know she's kinky–shouldn't she be too young to be kinky?--I'm picturing her with those pretty lips stretched around my–

Gospodi. I need to stop.

I really fucking wish she was the way I pictured her. Some quiet, shy, sheltered girl. One I would frighten a little but not harm in order to make her father suffer.

This girl, though?

She throws me off my game.

I didn't expect her to be hyper-sexual. Flirty. Wild and reckless. She's going to be harder to handle.

Or maybe easier, I can't tell yet.

Really, this is a gift. She wants me to take her home. Maybe she wants me to screw her. Wouldn't it be better if she were willing?

No! It's not.

I rub my forehead, scowling at the bus as it pulls up.

I wanted her *un*willing.

I planned to take photos of a frightened girl, tied up in compromised positions. I was going to tell Leon Poval I was doing every single terrible thing to his daughter that was done to Nadia, and if he wanted to see her alive, he would have to come and get her from me. In person.

So I can kill him.

I don't really know what to do with a girl like this. Letting her think, even for a night, that I am anything but vengeance seems like a cruel betrayal. For some reason, it seems worse than just stuffing her in the trunk of a car and telling her what's up from the start.

Dammit. I should've just let her suffer her own fate tonight at the party.

But no. I could never do that. What those *mudaks* were doing to her was a problem. She was about to be gang-raped in a corner from the way it looked to me. I may be willing to make Leon Poval believe I'm raping his daughter, but I'm not actually going to stand by and let it happen to her. That's a different thing entirely.

We climb on the bus, and I pay both our fares. I sit down, and Kat climbs onto my lap, making the other passengers on the bus look at us. Damn her. I don't need anyone remembering us. I firmly grip her hips and maneuver her to the seat beside me. "Be good," I admonish, trying to play her game.

She puts one fingertip up to her lips with a pout. "I thought I was being good." Her fingernails are short and unpainted, which seems at odds with the rest of her, which is done up. But then, my sense was this was a costume, not the real girl.

I pull my knit cap down and slouch in my seat. "Not on bus," I tell her gruffly.

For some reason, she eats it up. Maybe the molly is kicking in.

"You feel okay?"

"Aw." She reaches up to stroke my face, but I jerk back to forbid it. She goes on like nothing happened. "Somebody cares."

I fold my arms across my chest. "You're on my watch."

"For how long?" She takes the end of her braid and tickles my ear with it. This time I don't jerk away because it's obviously what she wants.

"You're going to get yourself spanked, little girl," I warn.

Her knees clap, and she sits higher in her seat like she just squeezed her buns together. There's no doubt in my mind now. She *fucking loves* domination.

I can work with this.

I think.

Hell, I don't know. I'm out of my depth, but I'm not going to stop or turn back. I'm also not gonna ask for help from Ravil or the cell. I know they'd give it to me. Advice, money, contacts, anything I needed. They'd probably get on a plane and fly here to lend their fists and muscle if I wanted.

But I don't want to involve them. This isn't a bratva war. It's personal. Poval is mine, and I intend to be the one to take him out. If there are repercussions, I'll be the one who suffers them. Alone.

"This is my stop." Kat tugs my sleeve.

I pretend to be surprised and follow her off. She holds a hand to her stomach, then turns and pukes in a bush.

Gross. But it gives me a chance to get control of her phone. I'd love to shut it off, so it can't be tracked. I take my jacket off her shoulders then divest her of the backpack purse, like I'm being helpful. I find a napkin in the pocket of my jacket, which I hand to her then slip my hand in her purse to shut down the phone.

"It's kicking in," she tells me cheerfully, as she wipes her mouth with the napkin, like puking is the gateway to fun.

I guess it would be.

"I wish you had some, too."

I grunt in response. I'm trying to figure out if I should just take her back to my place or go ahead with hers. Maybe I don't have to grab her tonight. Maybe I take her home and leave—just pick her back up in a couple of days when the ship is ready to sail.

I don't like that idea, though. She's seen my face. I need to control everything that happens beyond this point. No letting her tell her dad she met me or somehow looking me up. From this point forward, she's my prisoner.

Except the line seems fluid. From which point? Do I tie her up right now?

No, she's tripping. She won't be able to cause me any trouble now, and tying her up when she's rolling could make it a very bad trip. I know because they kept Nadia drugged most of her time, and her psychiatrist said it made the trauma worse because her reality was mixed in a dream-like state.

Okay, that's the plan, then. I'll take her to my place, make sure nothing happens while she's tripping, then tie her up in the morning.

"Hey, my place isn't far from here." I try to make my voice sound casual.

She bats her lashes at me. Literally. Bats them on purpose. "Are you inviting me over?"

"Yeah." I tip my head. "This way."

I take her to the small but bougie cottage I rented. I didn't need fancy, but it has all the things I require—proximity to Kateryna's apartment and a ground-floor private entrance, so I could stay low-key. Dima, our hacker, set it up for me using a wire deposit that can't be traced.

She comes in and looks around. It's a studio—the kind where the kitchen is just one wall and the bedroom is another, but everything's done in fine materials. Hardwood floors and granite countertops. I band an arm around her waist and pull her back against my front. "How do you like to be put to bed?" It's supposed to sound sexy but comes out as more of a gruff growl.

She rubs her soft ass against the front of my jeans. She smells like cherries and warm oatmeal cookies. That can't be right, but that's the impression I get. And underneath it, just pleasing female skin.

I bite her neck, and she shivers. She's dancing again, her lush body squirming and undulating in slo-mo like she's still up on that platform at the rave, turning on every guy in sight.

"Mmm," she hums softly.

Good. Her eyes are closed. She's not taking in the fact that I'm living out of a suitcase here.

Nothing to alert her to the fact that she just walked into the jaws of the trap I set for her.

Kat

Dy-ying.

I'm seriously dying. I finally found a real dom. The rush of love and well-being pouring into my brain from the hit of ecstasy makes this seem like I've just found Shangri La. But seriously. I feel like I have.

You're going to get yourself spanked, little girl.

I mean, how many times did I have to prance around in a schoolgirl outfit before some guy picked up the hint?

The trouble with men—boys, really. Let's face it, none of these guys are men—is that they see the sexy outfit and think it's for them. It's the whole male gaze thing. I learned about it in women's studies last semester—a class my dad said was bogus. So I'm playing to the male gaze. I'm giving them what they want to see from women. A sexual object to be desired. But I expect something in return.

More than a hit of ecstasy and a grope on the dance floor.

And it seems like this guy actually gets it.

Or maybe, I'm just twisting your basic alpha-hole into fantasy fodder. No. No, I'm not. He stepped in to rescue me. He was grumpy about it, but he did it. So he's not just a selfish prick like the rest of them.

Plus, he just asked me how I wanted to be put to bed. That may be the most positive sign yet.

I turn and remember that I have puke-breath. I cover my mouth with my hand. "I need a mint. Or mouthwash. Or a toothbrush, if you're willing to share."

"You don't need clean breath. I'm going to gag you." He watches me intently like he's gauging my reaction.

I look around, suddenly wondering if I've made a bad decision coming here. The place is gorgeous—small but posh and totally immaculate, not that it proves he's sane. Especially considering it's devoid of anything personal.

"Kidding." He takes his warm jacket off my shoulders

and tosses it onto the kitchen counter. "Unless you're into it." His voice is so low and gruff. Like a grumpy bear. I love it. "You can use my toothbrush." He takes my hand and leads me into the large, luxurious bathroom.

The cottage is lovely, and I'm rolling, so it feels almost magical. He puts toothpaste on his toothbrush while I lean against the wall and watch.

"Have you been here for long?"

"*Nyet.* It's a short-term rental. I'm passing through town." He hands me the toothbrush.

"What do you do?"

"I work in shipping."

I nod, not really absorbing his answer because I now have a close up view of his chest. It's as well-defined as I'd suspected. Since I have no filters at the moment—not that I have many when I'm sober—I let my fingertips slip under his black t-shirt to feel his skin.

He watches me darkly. No sign of approval. "Brush your teeth," he tells me.

My pussy clenches at the bossy command. I just might get spanked tonight! It's looking good for me. I grin and start brushing.

He stands at the granite counter watching me, even though the normal thing to do would be to offer me some privacy in case I have to pee or something.

I finish brushing and rinse my mouth out. "Much better. Are you going to let me touch you now?"

His brows pop like he finds my request unexpected.

I bunch his shirt up in my fist and try to pull him closer, but he catches my wrist. "You like to be in charge, Kat?"

Several things hit me at once. One is the visceral reaction to his touch—the flush of heat, the desire to feel even more of that controlling strength. Then there's the stern tone—it makes my knees weak. But also, *he said my name.*

"What did you call me?"

Nothing changes in his face. It feels like he takes him a long time to answer, but time gets wonky when you're rolling. "What is your name? I thought that *mudak* at the rave called you Kat?"

Oh, right. That makes sense. I bob my head in agreement. "Kateryna. Kat. Kit-Kat. What's your name?"

He locks eyes with me like it's important. "Adrian." Still holding my wrists, he propels me backward out the bathroom door and into the tiny bedroom / living room combo. "You haven't answered any of my questions, *dietka.*"

"I forgot what they were." I'm breathless. Horny. Madly in love. But that's the molly talking.

"I asked if you like to be in charge."

"I *am* in charge," I sass him, shaking my hands free to put them on my hips. It's true–I hold the power until I choose to surrender it. That's what I told Delaney when she questioned my taste in sexual encounters.

He frowns. "I should have gagged you from the start," he says, but he doesn't move to overpower me. I still get the feeling he's watching for my reaction to his words.

I giggle and attempt to slide both my hands up his shirt again. "Maybe you should try," I purr.

He spins me around and claps a hand over my mouth, yanking my body against his.

I squeal my thrill against his hand.

"Like this, *dietka*? You like a little struggle? Hmm. Do you want to be overpowered?"

I wrestle him.

He brings his lips to my ear. "I need a real answer." His tone is stern. "*Yes* or *no*." He lifts his fingers partway off my mouth.

"Yes."

"Yes, you want me to take charge?"

"Yes, Daddy."

"Don't call me *Daddy*."

I turn around to face him again. "Should I call you *sir*?"

"Not that, either. *On your knees.*"

I almost orgasm from the command. I love his accent—it somehow makes him sound grumpier. Sensations are so heightened right now, I'm two strokes away from a full-body climax.

I drop to my knees and quickly work the button on his jeans. He settles one hand behind my head in a cradling way that gets me even more excited. I free his erection and take his thick length into my mouth. I wish I had more finesse, but I'm a little sloppy in general right now. Hopefully, I'll make up for it with enthusiasm. I suction my lips around the head of his dick, tasting a drop of his salty essence.

"Yum," I say, popping off.

I bring my free hand between my legs because I need to come so badly.

Adrian's eyes darken, and his fingers tighten around my head, driving me forward over his cock again. "Good girl."

Good girl! My nipples tighten in my blouse. The words are magical to me. All I ever wanted to be called, despite my efforts at playing the bad girl.

I bob over his cock, in and out, taking him right to the back of my throat every time, sucking hard, swirling my tongue on the underside. I shove my fingers inside my panties to stroke my own flesh.

I must get too enthusiastic because he grunts, "Careful with the teeth."

"Sorry," I gasp. "Sor—"

He interrupts my apology by putting his cock back in

my mouth. His grip at the base of my skull is firm without being rough. Controlling without inciting resistance. I really, really like this guy.

I don't think it's just the molly talking. He feels like a match. The fulfillment to all my fantasies of being dominated.

I give the blowjob my all. Even though I'm really turned on, I can't quite make him get to the finish line. That's how it is with ecstasy though. You're already so happy, it's hard to make the explosion go off. Not that I'm a huge user. This is my fourth time ever, and I've been on the party scene since I was fifteen.

I sit back on my heels, losing focus.

"You okay?" Adrian strokes the pad of his thumb down my cheek.

"Yeah. Just thirsty."

And that's when I know he's the right guy. Because he puts his erection away–as painful as it must be–he shoves it back in his pants and zips up–and goes to get me water.

I kick off my shoes and sit cross-legged on his bed where he brings me a filled glass.

"How long will it last?" he asks.

"The ecstasy?" I ask, gulping down the water. "A couple hours. Why?"

He stabs his fingers through his dark hair. "I'm taking advantage. It's wrong."

Aw. How sweet. Grumpy bear *does* have a hero complex. I totally called it. But he's also dommy. A perfect combination. Except now I'm going to have to talk him into continuing.

"Don't worry. It's not like alcohol," I say. "It's more like heightened sensations, not lowered inhibitions."

He glowers at me with brows drawn. Grumpy hero bear.

I'm in love. With him. With this moment. This experience.

He takes the empty glass from my hand and sets it down then squats in front of me, pushing my knees wide. "So how did you want to be put to bed?"

Oh damn. He's so sexy. Sinfully sexy. He runs his hands up the outsides of my thighs, sliding them under my skirt. His thumbs trace light circles at my inner thighs, close to the edge of my panties.

I open my mouth to say it, but no words come out.

I'm a bold girl. My dad calls me spoiled.

I'm not afraid of much of anything. But this is embarrassing. And I might hate the result.

Adrian stops advancing when I don't speak, raising his brows in that authoritative manner he has. "Tell me, *malysh*."

The word is close enough to the Ukranian that I can guess at its meaning–*baby*. Not *kid* this time.

I melt a little. Or maybe those are my panties catching fire.

"W-with a little…spanking?" I have to force the last word across my lips. It's embarrassing as hell, but he doesn't laugh.

He also doesn't seem surprised. "You *were* a bad girl."

A laugh bursts out of me, relief and pleasure that he's running with this. I'm also terrified. I've never gotten a guy to give me more than a couple slaps. What if it hurts too much, and I hate it?

He tips his head toward the middle of the bed. "Hands and knees."

Oh God! Oh goodie! Wait…am I doing this? My heart flops around erratically in my chest.

I'm totally doing this. I crawl onto the comfortable bed on my hands and knees and look over my shoulder at him.

"I'll go slow. You say *stop* if you need me to, yes?"

More love pours into my heart. Gratitude. Joy. This guy is so perfect.

"Okay."

He lifts my short, pleated skirt and lays it on my back. "I like your panties."

I crane my head to look over my shoulder to see if he's making fun of me. "They go with the outfit," I say defensively.

Instead of sexy panties–lace or satin or a minuscule thong–I'm wearing chaste white practical panties. Because I'm supposed to be an innocent schoolgirl.

"Oh, I get that." He gives my ass a smack, and I yelp.

Wow. Ouch. Yep, heightened sensations mean it hurts way more.

He grips the place he smacked and squeezes then releases the flesh and rubs. "It's cute." He slaps the back of my thigh, underneath the panties. I yelp even louder.

"Quiet, Kateryna, or I will have to gag you. I don't want the neighbors hearing."

"If you gag me, how will you hear me say *stop*?"

"I wouldn't. A good reason for you to obey, then, isn't it?" He smacks my other cheek.

"Ow! Not so hard."

He hooks his thumbs under the waistband of my panties and tugs them down my thighs.

I stiffen, expecting another smack, but he strokes my ass, trailing his roughened palm lightly across my skin. After a moment, I relax. My skin tingles in the three places he's slapped me, and it's starting to heat and burn a little. His light touch only makes me hungry for the harsher treatment again.

He strokes along the inside of one cheek, following it up to the cleft of my ass then sliding down the center between my legs. He gives my pussy a few light slaps. Heat explodes in my core. I suddenly want more. I chase his fingers, pushing my hips back.

He rubs between my legs with bold, firm strokes.

I moan loudly to show my appreciation.

"*Quiet*, Kateryna."

I love the way he uses my full name like I'm in trouble. It's so hot.

He gives my pussy another slap.

This time I make a plaintive sound. I reach between my legs to stroke myself.

"You rub, *malysh*. I'll spank."

"Wait—"

He slaps my bare ass, but it's a good one. Slappy and firm without making me yelp.

"Mmm," I moan, rubbing the pad of my index finger through my juices. I don't usually get that wet, but apparently, all I was missing before was a hot dommy man slapping my ass. Everything feels so wet and swollen down there, I don't even recognize my own anatomy.

True to his word, Adrian goes slowly. He slaps one side, rubs. Slaps the other. Repeats. It's a perfect pace for my attention-wandering mind and the intensity is just right for my overly sensitive state, too.

Now, if I could just come. I change hands when my arm gets tired of holding me up. Adrian pushes my torso down so my chest is on the bed and my ass still in the air, which is actually easier. The change was needed, too, because I was beginning to space out.

He picks up speed with the spanking. My whole ass is warm now, so the slaps don't feel so intense when they fall. It all feels wonderful. I love it. But I still can't seem to make myself come, as much as I want to.

"I'm sorry," I croak after a few minutes. Or maybe an

hour. I don't know—time is weird right now. "I can't come."

"Maybe you won't," Adrian says, like it doesn't matter. "Does it feel good?"

"Yes."

He grips my ankle and pulls one leg long and then the other until I'm on my belly. Then he rolls me over and takes my lowered panties off.

I figure he's going to have sex with me, and I'm getting ready to ask if he has a condom, but instead, he parts my legs and pushes my knees up, settling between them.

"Oh!" I clutch his head when he licks into me, pulling his hair with the glory of it.

He lifts his face. "*Quiet.*"

"Sorry, sorry!" I whisper-pant. "Don't stop. Please don't stop."

"You don't have to come," he tells me, tracing his tongue around the inside of my labia.

"I will," I threaten, my inner thighs starting to shake and shiver.

I chase his mouth with my hips, desperate for more. He penetrates me with his tongue, but it's not enough. I pull his mouth against me, seeking more. He finds the spot that drives me wild—is that my clit? How embarrassing that I don't even know. All I know is that it's driving me crazy.

Adrian screws one finger inside me, then another. He pumps them in and out while he continues to lick and suck what must be my clit.

I don't realize I'm crying out until Adrian lifts his head and growls, "Cover your mouth, Kateryna."

I slap a hand over my mouth as a feverish heat flushes over me. And then I come. It's momentous. Monumental. Mind-blowing.

By far the best orgasm I've ever had. My internal muscles clamp down on his fingers and pulses of energy shoot down my inner thighs, straight to the soles of my feet where my toes curl. My pelvis jumps and shakes and rocks on the bed. Adrian never stops flicking his tongue over my most sensitive nub while he pumps his fingers in and out.

I let out a long low moan as I come down the other side of it, my belly shaking, my knees flapping against Adrian's shoulders.

"No more," I whimper because it's suddenly too much. Terribly intense. I feel like I'm flying and also like I need to cry. Oh wait–I am crying.

He stops immediately, slipping his fingers out and stroking my thigh with one of his large hands. *"Blyad'.* What happened? Are you okay?"

"I'm fine," I gasp, rolling to my side to hide my face in my hands. Embarrassing!

He clasps my shoulder. His hand is warm and comforting. I like it far too much.

"It's good. It was so good," I reassure him.

"This is the molly?"

"Yeah." I nod and sniff. It's real. The experience is real, the emotions are real. They're just heightened. Amplified.

He moves away, which is both relieving and disappointing. I hear the click of something, but I don't look, I'm too lost in my own world. He brings me another glass of water and puts me under the covers. "Go to sleep now, *dietka.*"

I'm not sleepy, but I'm completely wrung out, so I take his advice and close my eyes.

I'm totally blissed out. Relaxed.

I let sleep seep in, never guessing that in the morning I would wake tied to the bed with a gag in my mouth.

That standing above me would be the guy I thought was a prince the night before, taking photos of me in a compromised position with his phone.

3

Adrian

I wait until Kat is sound asleep, then I grab her purse and search it. She has a bottle of CBD gummies. That could come in handy. Especially for getting her onto the ship—a problem I haven't solved yet.

I take the phone out of her bag and bring it to the kitchen with the laptop Dima gave me. I text Dima for assistance. He calls immediately. I pick up in a hushed voice, but Kat doesn't even stir.

"I have the girl," I tell Dima in Russian. He's the only one I've been in contact with about my plans, and that's because I need him. I don't want to involve the rest of my cell. This isn't their fight.

"I thought you weren't grabbing her until tomorrow."

"Plans changed," I say simply. "I have her phone shut off to avoid tracking. What do I do now?"

Dima walks me through disconnecting the location tracker then opening the phone up to search for any additional trackers. I don't find any, which seems careless on

Poval's part. "All right, now connect the phone to the laptop, so I can access all the data."

I do as Dima instructs.

"Turn it on, and I can grab everything."

I power the phone back up and watch the screen run through a series of download commands and lists of files scrolling rapidly. While it's working, I thumb through her contacts.

"She has *Papa* listed in her contacts," I tell Dima.

"Beautiful. Let me see." I hear the clack of keys as he accesses the information. "I'll try to trace it to a location. It might be a while."

The upload to Dima's system ends. "Now what?" I ask.

"Now you destroy that phone."

"How will I send him the message that I have her?"

"I can send messages using her number that will route from random servers across the globe. Are you ready to send one now?"

I consider. I took a photo of her when she was hiding her face and crying after her orgasm. It showed her bare, reddened ass red and without context, definitely looked non-consensual. Like she was suffering, not riding the high of orgasm.

I glance over at her sleeping form on the bed. I could easily get some more photos that appear compromising right now and send them over.

But the moment I send them, the hunt for Kat will begin, and I can't get on that cargo ship for thirty-some hours. It will be harder to keep her hidden here, so close to her home.

"Not yet," I tell him. "Can I just text the message to you when I'm ready?"

"That works. Listen, Adrian…"

"*Da?*"

"Ravil wants you to report. He said you're not answering his messages."

I grind my teeth. Disobeying my *pakhan* feels wrong, especially after all Ravil has done for me. I try to explain. "I don't want to involve the cell. This is personal. I only asked for your help because, well–"

"Yeah, I know. You can't do this part alone. I think the point is that you can't do any of this alone. Ravil will have your back, too. You know that, right?"

"I can't involve him," I say fiercely. "It's not right."

"Well, you need to tell him that yourself. He doesn't like being blown off."

"Yes, I will." It's a lie. I'm not going to contact Ravil. The less he knows, the better. "Thank you, Dima."

"Of course. You're a brother, Adrian. Whatever you need, I've got you."

I swallow down the lump in my throat. The bratva didn't take my soul, like it does to most men. It returned me to humanity.

Searching for Nadia turned me into an animal. I used up my money to get to America, where I only had a thin lead on Poval. I knew Maykl from my home town–he was a friend of a friend–and I made contact.

Ravil instantly brought me into the fold. Gave me a place to stay and put me to work. Made me a brother. Maxim, the bratva fixer, trained me to be the cleaner. The guy who wipes a scene of all traces of violence, all clues to the crime. No, the work isn't legal, but I didn't care then and I don't care now. I didn't plan on operating within the lines of any law.

Ravil helped me find Poval and eventually Nadia. When I was arrested after burning the factory to the ground, he paid for the best defense attorney in Chicago to defend me. I owe him everything. I've pledged my life to the bratva and have zero regrets.

"Thank you," I say and hang up.

I retrieve the zip ties from my suitcase, but I can't bring myself to wake Kat by putting them on her yet. Instead, I lie down beside her to catch a few hours of sleep before everything turns rancorous between us.

$\approx$

Adrian

In the morning, I zip tie Kat's wrists together and then attach them to a chain of zip ties around the headboard. Using a strip off one of my t-shirts, I tie a gag around her head to cover her mouth. Kat sleeps through the whole thing.

I get out my phone and take some more photos. Leon Poval will lose his shit when he sees them.

Kat will probably lose her shit when she wakes up, too, which can't be helped. I knew it would be hard to carry out, but it's worse than I imagined. I never planned on actually having sex with her. Only staging photos to look like she'd been abused.

Not that I fucked her. I didn't even come. I keep telling myself that to make myself feel better.

The truth is, I'm sick as hell over this shit.

But I knew it wouldn't be easy. I vowed to do my best to keep her comfortable and unharmed.

She wakes up and screams. I snap another photo because her terror is too genuine not to pass along to her dear father. Then I tuck my phone in my back pocket and walk over to her. "Hush, *dietka*. Be a good girl, and you won't get hurt."

That only pisses her off. Calling her *good girl* might have worked last night, but she's definitely not into it now. She kicks her heels and writhes on the bed, making her short skirt ride up her waist even more. Her panties are still off, and I have to force myself not to look at that pretty pussy she let me taste. She sports a neat trim over her mons, the rest waxed bare.

Fuck. Why did I have to taste her? Why did I mix business with pleasure?

It was a monumental mistake because I have this huge urge to try to make everything better for her now, but of course, I can't.

She shouts something from behind the gag. Fear is kicking in, and her panic appears to be overtaking the anger.

"Listen." I sit on the bed beside her and cage her throat in my hand. She fights against me, trashing, eyes wide with terror. "*Listen* to me, *dietka.*"

She stops moving and hyperventilates against the gag, the whites of her eyes showing.

"I'm taking off the gag. You're going to keep quiet. Don't make me squeeze." I pulse my fingers around her neck, so she understands what I mean.

She continues her wild, frantic breathing.

"Okay? Are you going to keep quiet?"

She nods her head jerkily.

I grab the remote control by the bed and turn on the large flat-screen television mounted to the opposite wall, cranking the volume in case she tunes up again. The moment the gag comes off she spits, "Pervert! You sick bastard. Did you take a picture of me like this? What in the—"

I clamp my hand back over her mouth to shut her up. "I'm not a pervert. This is business." I deliver the words in a business-like manner. Emotionless, the way Maxim or Ravil would.

I test removing my hand again.

"What business? Pornography? Prostitution?" Then terror replaces the anger again. "What are you going to do with me?"

"Nothing. I don't rape women."

"No, you just tie them up and take dirty photos for other perverts like you?"

Fuck.

I should put the gag back in. Walk away.

Better yet, I should keep her drugged until we get on the ship. That's what they did to Nadia.

But I don't know anything about drugging women. What if I fucked it up? She still has the MDMA in her system from last night. I don't know if there are drug interactions that might occur.

But I don't gag her or walk away. I'm an idiot. Instead, I pick up the glass of water beside the bed and hold it to her lips. She has to be dehydrated.

She takes a swallow, then spits the water in my face.

"Okay, you're done." I wrap the gag back around her head. When I lean forward to tie it, she headbutts me in the nose.

I rear back in pain, blood gushing down my shirt.

"Help me! Hel–"

I clap a hand over her mouth to cut off her screams. My other hand wraps around her throat. "Shut up," I snarl.

She fights me.

I tighten my fingers around her neck. I'm not cutting off her oxygen, but I show her that I could.

After a moment of trying to shake my grip, she breaks, sobbing against my hand.

"Not a fucking sound," I warn her. I'm bleeding all over both of us.

She keeps crying.

All right. It's fine. I expected tears. I steel myself against them, making my expression ugly. "Scream again, and I'll stop your breath. Understand?"

She nods against my hand. I release her mouth and use the hem of my t-shirt to staunch the flow of blood from my nose, one hand remaining caged around her throat.

She's still crying. Not quiet, sniffling cries, but out-of-control sobbing. It seems like she's winding herself up rather than getting something out.

I have plenty of experience with female tears. My sister soaks her pillow nearly every night with them.

"You're okay. Listen to me, Kateryna. If you do as you're told, you'll get out of this unharmed."

She focuses on my face, taking deep, gulping breaths. "G-get out of what?"

Blyad'. I should just keep my mouth shut. The less I tell her, the better.

"Wh-what are you going to do with me?"

I bring the sides of my thumbs to my nose to feel if it's crooked, but it feels okay.

"I'm going to be sick," she moans.

It might be a trick, but I believe her. She puked last night in the bushes and hasn't had anything to eat since. Plus, she's completely overwrought.

I curse and cut the plastic zip tie holding her wrists to the headboard with my penknife.

She pukes down the front of herself before I can get her up.

Fuck.

"All right," I say, pulling her off the bed and onto her feet. Her wrists are still manacled together with another zip tie, but considering what she's already done with her skull and her voice, I brace myself for anything she might try.

She seems docile now, though. More upset about the vomit down the front of her than her current situation.

"Let's clean you up."

I would put her over my shoulder, but I'm afraid she'll vomit down my back. Instead, I propel her to the bathroom, holding her wrists with one hand and guiding her back with the other.

In the bathroom, she goes right for the toilet, dropping to sit on it and peeing as she cries softly. I grab some toilet paper and shove it up my nostril to stop the bleeding then wet a washcloth and wait for her to finish. She uses her bound hands to get some toilet paper.

"Does this turn you on?" she demands as she attempts to wipe herself using both hands. Her skirt gets in the way, so I lift it for her.

"*Nyet.*"

I flush the toilet for her and tug her up to stand, so I can clean her up.

"Let me go. Please."

"I will let you go when my business is complete."

"What business? What was the picture for?"

I mop her white blouse with the washcloth, turning it translucent. She has mess down her cleavage, and I work the washcloth between her breasts. They're full and soft. The asshole in me wishes I'd seen them last night. Before we turned adversarial.

She grabs my wrist and brings her knee up, trying to nail my balls.

I sidestep and snatch her by her throat, pressing her up against the wall. "*Don't,*" I warn.

She tries to knee me again, and I have to really cut off her air. She chokes and gasps, eyes bulging.

I hold her another moment to really instill fear in her, then I relax. "Knock it off, or you'll spend the next two weeks tied spreadeagle to a bed."

She studies me, her cornflower blue eyes ticking back and forth on mine. "Why two weeks? What's happening?"

I release her throat and pull her away from the wall. "Back to the bed. You're being a pain in my ass."

"You're being a royal dick," she shoots back.

She's not wrong. I take her back to the bed and reattach the zip tie that pulls her wrists over her head and connects them to the headboard.

I take each of her ankles and attach them to the foot of the bed spreadeagle. Then, because the sight turns my stomach, I take another photo. If it makes me sick, it will definitely destroy her dad.

~

Kat

"You *bastard*!"

Adrian—if that's really his name—pockets his phone. "Are you going to keep your mouth shut, or do I need to put the gag back on?"

I try to kick my legs, which only succeeds in making the zip ties dig into the skin around my ankles. I'm scared—more scared than I've ever been in my life—but I'm also pissed.

This guy is a psychopath. He lured me into his place and then trapped me.

No, that doesn't fit. He did lure me to his place and trap me, but there's something rational and non-psychopathic about him. But it wasn't him calling this *business* because what kind of non-psychopathic person kidnaps women and zip ties them to beds for work?

"Go fuck yourself, fuck-face." Yep. I'm very mature right now.

He seems to take the fact that I haven't screamed again as evidence of my cooperation because he goes into the kitchen. I watch as he scrambles four eggs and makes four slices of buttered toast.

"I have a history test today," I remember. I also had studio time booked to work on my pottery.

"You're going to miss it." He piles them all on a plate and returns to the bed, standing over me.

"I will be missed," I say, even though I'm not positive it's true. I don't have any good friends. The ones I had in prep school were circumstantial. They've gone off to uni now. No one stayed in Liverpool. There's no one in my classes who would miss me.

The art teacher won't think anything of me missing my timeslot on the wheel. I can be flaky.

The food smells good, despite the fact that my stomach is upset.

"I'll cut your ankles free if you promise to be good."

"I'll be good," I lie.

I probably should've tried to scream for help again while he was in the kitchen. I'm not sure what stopped me— whether it was his threat to choke me, or the fact that I don't quite believe his threat. I mean, I do. He did stop my breath in the bathroom for a few terrifying seconds. My neck still hurts from where he held me. He's definitely capable of murder.

But his violence seems measured. He didn't hit me back when I headbutted him. Nor did he retaliate much in the bathroom.

He sets the plate of eggs and toast on the bedside table and cuts one of the zip ties with a pocket knife then picks up my panties. "Kick me, and I'll take a belt to your ass," he warns.

It makes me want to kick him. So hard. Especially because it makes me feel squirmy inside. Like, under different circumstances, I might want him to carry through on a threat like that. If it was my choice. Not when I'm tied up against my will.

But the food smells good, and I don't want him to hurt me, so I lie still and watch as he slips my free foot through the hole of my panties before he cuts the other ankle free and feeds it through.

It's not sexy. I mean, it shouldn't be. But I get all fluttery and weird as he drags the panties up my thighs. I want him to be the guy I thought he was last night.

Was I just completely out of my mind on ecstasy? Or was he really amazing? I know at the time I felt like I'd hit the jackpot.

Needing to somehow recapture that dynamic, needing to push this out of the terror realm and into something else, I push through my feet to lift my hips for him to pull my panties over my ass, and when he's over me, I roll my hips.

It works. He stalls for a brief second, and his brows dip as he yanks my panties the rest of the way up. He pushes my hips down. "You are crazy girl." His accent is thick this morning.

"That's funny. I was thinking you were the psychopath here."

"No. Not psychopath." He sits beside me on the bed and picks up the plate. He scoops a forkful of eggs, and I open my mouth. "You are not what I expected."

I close my mouth and turn my head to the side to refuse the food. "Wait…what?"

He eats the bite of eggs himself. "It's not poisoned. I

won't hurt you if you cooperate." He catches my eye and holds my gaze like he really wants me to believe him.

"Is this…personal?" I ask, my voice quavering. "Do you know me?"

"I know your father." He holds another bite out of me. I want the food, but the information is more important. Again, I turn away.

"Hang on. Do you *work for* my father?"

Now it's his turn to be flabbergasted. He stares at me with his mouth open. "Work for him? You think one of your father's men would do this to the boss's daughter–" he breaks off and shakes his head. "Yes, they probably would. They are the worst scum on the Earth."

My heart pounds with this new knowledge.

"You're holding me hostage." I'm catching up.

"*Da.*"

"He will kill you." I say it not as a threat but with total sincerity. My father is a ruthless businessman. He thinks I don't know he's a crime lord, but I'm not stupid. I know everyone around him lives in fear. I have long believed my mother abandoned me to save her own life. Or maybe that's just what a girl of six tells herself when her mother disappears one day.

A story that ends in a happy ending at a later date. My mother returning to me when she can. Reclaiming her beloved daughter.

But, of course, she never came.

Maybe she's dead.

Maybe he killed her.

"He will want me dead," Adrian agrees like he's content with this knowledge.

A cold chill runs across my skin. "Are you asking for ransom?"

Adrian hesitates. "Yes."

More cold prickles shoot down my spine. There's something more to this. "What is the ransom?" My words come out as barely more than a whisper.

He stares at me like he's not sure about his choice. "Five million."

"Five million?" I sound shrill. "Is that all? You know he has at least a hundred million, right?" I know because I heard him bragging to a woman about it once.

"He has to bring the money himself." There's something terribly sinister about the way Adrian says the words, and I suddenly realize what this is: a trap.

And I'm the bait.

I glance at the plate of food and lift my chin at him. He takes the hint and feeds me a bite. I'm instantly starving. I chew quickly, swallow and gesture with my eyes again. He feeds me one bite after the next until I've finished half the eggs and two pieces of toast. I eye a third piece. "Is that yours?"

"You can have it. You're not going to puke again, are you?"

"No. I feel better." I eat half of the third piece of toast and then quit, turning my face away from him. He cleans the plate of what's left.

I've had time to digest the information while I ate. "Are you in law enforcement?"

He scoffs.

"Didn't think so. So… this is personal?"

He gives a single nod. "It's personal."

"He killed someone you love."

"*Nyet.*"

"No?" I'm surprised. I thought for sure that would be it. Why else would someone have a personal vendetta against a man?

"No."

"What did he do?"

"You don't want to know." Adrian gets up.

My body reacts to his loss with panic. "Wait. Come back."

He stops and turns but doesn't sit down again. "What is it?"

"You want to hurt my dad? I'm in."

He goes still, his face an inscrutable mask. "That's good," he says after a beat, but I get the feeling he doesn't believe me. Of course, he doesn't. It could easily be a ploy. I mean, maybe it is a ploy on my part. I just want to get out of these horrible zip ties. I want to have a hot shower and change my clothes. But I'm not exactly loyal to my dad. I hate him in that angry, unloved teenager way. The one where part of me still desperately wants his love and approval, and the rest of me hates him because I know I'll never get it.

I stare at Adrian's strong muscled back when he walks away, taking the empty plate to the kitchen. He washes it and puts it in the drying rack.

"Is Adrian your real name?" I call to his back.

"*Da*. Adrian Turgenev," he tells me, like it's important. It also implies that he's not afraid of anyone finding out his identity–not my father. Not the authorities.

So, either he thinks it won't matter, or he doesn't care. Maybe because he doesn't plan on letting me live.

"Are you going to kill me?" I blurt.

"No." He's doing grumpy bear again. "I told you. I–"

"--won't hurt me if I do what I'm told."

"Precisely this." He nods.

This time I believe him. Things are coming into focus. Some of my worst fears have been allayed. He's not a psychopath who plans to torture me and keep me in a cage as his personal slave. *God! Why does that thought sort of turn me on? Maybe Delaney's right. There is something sick in me that requires healing.* He's not going to sell me at a slave auction. He doesn't plan to kill me for his revenge on my father.

Adrian's phone rings, and he pulls it out of his pocket. "Nadia." He turns his back to me, speaking in Russian. His voice is soft. Coaxing.

I go cold.

For some reason, this unpleasant shock rivals waking up with a gag in my mouth.

Adrian has a woman.

4

Adrian

"How are you?" I ask my younger sister in our mother tongue. I try to talk to her every day or two. The whole time I've been gone, I've battled guilt over leaving her there alone. She's come a long way in the year since she's been free, but she still has bouts of debilitating paranoia and depression brought on by her PTSD. She suffers from agoraphobia–fear of leaving the house. She's getting counseling, but I'm still so afraid she'll relapse.

"I'm fine." She gives a groggy laugh. "I just woke up. It's six a.m. here. You texted me to call when I woke up."

"Right, sorry. Have you left the building since we last talked?"

"No, but I'm going out tonight."

Right. It's Thursday, which means Story's band is playing.

Nadia's not entirely alone in America. We live in the Kremlin. Not the real Kremlin, but the lakeshore Chicago high rise owned by Ravil, my bratva *pakhan*. The neighbors call the building the Kremlin because only Russians live there. Unless you count Ravil's lawyer wife—the one who got me off on the arson charges after I burned down Poval's sofa factory which was really a sex trafficking front.

Oleg's American girlfriend, Story, also lives there.

I grit my teeth. I should be thrilled any time Nadia's willing to leave the apartment. It took me months and months just to get her out of the building. But I fear she's more than a little fixated on Story's younger brother, Flynn who plays in the band. And Flynn is a fucking player.

He's the last guy my sister needs to throw herself at. Although, that might be the saving grace. Flynn is too busy with all the fangirls throwing their panties on stage at him to pay any attention to my socially phobic, extremely damaged sister.

"Is Sasha going?" I don't want her there if there's not another woman.

"Yes. Sasha and Maxim, Oleg, and Maykl."

"Good. If you need to leave early, you tell Maykl, and he'll take you back." Maykl promised me he'd look after Nadia while I was gone. He's the bratva brother I knew from Russia. Newer to our cell, like me. Honorable. I trust him with her. Also, I told him I'd cut off his balls if he touched her, so there's that.

"I…I think I will stay."

Fuck. I fear she's really obsessed with Flynn. Should I say something? I should. I need to warn her that he's a heartbreaker.

No, I can't bring myself to. It's the first interest she's shown in anything since Poval kidnapped her from home almost two years ago. And if this gets her out of the building, it has to be a win. I just fear a heartbreak would be the end of her.

Literally.

She was suicidal for a long time.

"You're going to work today?"

"Of course," she chides me. "You think I can't make it to work because you're gone?"

"I'm just making sure."

Ravil, in all his benevolence, magically found work for my sister when I finally found her and brought her back with me. Just like he took me in and showed me the ropes when I arrived in Chicago, following the trail that led me to the sofa factory, he found a place for Nadia.

Since she's still learning English and is afraid to interact with people, he gave her a job cleaning the Kremlin. Never mind that he already has at least five other Russian immigrants on the payroll for the same job.

Now that she's coming out of her depression, she does a little babysitting for him as well.

"You've showered?" Sometimes personal hygiene goes out the window when she's in a funk.

"I will shower after work."

Right. She wouldn't go out to see the Storytellers without showering.

"Eaten breakfast?"

"I will. Adrian, I'm fine. What about you? What are you doing? When are you coming home?"

"I just have some business to take care of. I'll be back in a couple weeks... if it all goes well."

"And if it doesn't?" Her voice is tight with strain.

"Don't worry about me," I tell her. I don't intend to die at Poval's hand. I know it's a distinct possibility, but I plan on making it home alive. With justice served.

I sneak a look at Kat, who doesn't deserve her role in my vengeance. She's frantically working her wrists against the zip ties.

"Ravil wants you to call him. He said it's important."

"Yeah, I will. I have to go, Nadia. Call me tomorrow when you wake."

"I will."

I hesitate. "Have a good time tonight."

"*Spasibo*," she thanks me. "*Do svidaniya.*"

"*Do svidaniya.*" I say goodbye and hang up then walk to Kat's side. "*Hey*," I say sharply. "You're only hurting yourself. You won't get free. Stop trying."

"Go fuck yourself, *mudak*."

Asshole is the same in Ukrainian as it is in Russian.

I don't have a thing for hurting women. In fact, it's the opposite. Knowing what my sister suffered, the idea of hurting a woman makes me sick. But Kat looks so beautiful right now with her wrists tied over her head. Her lips are chapped which makes them red and pretty and very kissable.

I rub my forehead.

I shouldn't be getting emotionally involved with this girl. That should be the farthest thing from my mind right now. I should be channeling Ravil's cool business-like approach. Show nothing, give nothing. But instead I find the need to claim this girl. To comfort her. To show her who's boss in a sexier way than using zip ties on her poor wrists. The way she liked it last night.

Katerina is a beautiful, sexy girl, and last night definitely tweaked me in a way I didn't expect. I may have not thought I had a thing for the school girl outfit or playing dominant, but now I do. Now I definitely do. I will never forget what it felt like to make her come all over my fingers after spanking that pretty little ass red.

"They hurt," she complains. "My arms hurt. My wrists hurt. I can't be in this position any longer!"

Da. She's right. I need to change things. I pull my pen

knife out of my pocket and cut the zip tie around her wrists loose, catching her hands to keep her from hitting me.

And she does try. She hits and kicks at me, suddenly a violent little ball of venom. I have to pin her down on the bed, my knees straddling her waist, my weight falling into manacling her wrists with my hands. I sit on her pelvis to pin her down.

After a moment of useless struggle, she goes still, breathing hard beneath me. Her gaze is less angry than it is...*hurt?*

This is why I shouldn't have mixed business with pleasure. I am fucking this up so badly.

"Let me go." Her eyes fill with angry tears.

"Don't make this hard, *dietka*."

She changes tack. "I need to use the loo."

It's probably a lie, but what can I do? I'm not going to make her soil the bed. "Okay. Let's go." I should put the zip ties back on her, but I decide to take the risk and just hang onto her. She's small and not trained in hand to hand combat like I am. She could get lucky and take me out, but it seems highly unlikely.

I ease my hips up from hers and swing a leg off the bed, tug her by her wrists to pivot her up to sit then stand. Her glare still holds the same hurt I saw a moment ago.

I fold her wrists behind her back one at a time then turn her to face the bathroom and walk behind her, holding her prisoner.

When we get to the bathroom, she uses the toilet then turns on the shower. "I feel gross," she says sulkily. Without looking at me, she starts stripping off her clothes, starting with her knee-high socks.

I shut the door and lean my ass against it. "Fine. Use shower." I fold my arms over my chest.

There's no window in the shower. She's not getting out. It seems harmless enough.

She unzips her skirt and lets it drop, then she takes off the blouse, her bra, and finally her panties.

I try to keep my gaze... well, diffused. I can't very well look away or turn my back. She might bash my head in with the back of the ceramic toilet tank. But it's damn hard not to appreciate her beautiful body. She has full, ripe breasts that contrast with her tiny rib cage and narrow waist. Not much in the hips department, but her legs are shapely, and that ass...so cute.

She ignores me and pulls off the elastic bands holding the ends of her braids to unwind her long dark hair. She steps into the shower and slides the frosted glass door closed.

"Don't you have any conditioner?" she demands.

"*Nyet.* Why would I need conditioner?"

"*I* need conditioner. Do you know how tangled my hair is going to be?"

"Sorry, *printsessa.*"

She whips the shower door open to flip me the bird. I give her a hard look even though her brat act is totally growing on me. She slides the door closed again, but not before I get an eyeful of her wet body, even more glorious with droplets of water dripping down, begging to be licked.

Damn.

She's in there forever. I think about telling her to hurry the fuck up, but what does it matter, really? This is the only chance she'll get to be free of the zip ties, I might as well let her enjoy it.

"Who is Nadia?" she demands after a stretch. I hear the accusation in her voice.

Suddenly, the hurt in her eyes and voice makes more sense.

Fuck.

That means she's already attached to me. Attached enough to be jealous of a girl who calls me on the phone.

Why did I have to get sexual with her last night?

I don't need this complication.

She doesn't need this complication. Or does it make it easier? No, that was my thinking last night. Get her to my place consensually to avoid further trauma. But it's really more of a delayed trauma.

Because ultimately, there's one way this ends: with her father dead by my hand.

How's she going to feel about that if she thinks we're friends? Lovers?

I don't answer, turning the angles over in my mind. I'm not practiced yet at making split-second decisions. I'm the cleaner. The one who thinks through things after they happen. I take time to chew over a situation.

Suddenly, she flies out of the still-running shower, the handle of my razor clutched like a weapon. She leaps on me, straddling my waist, and tries to drive the handle of the razor into my eye. I catch her wrist, which is slippery and wet and storm forward into the shower, where I pin her back against the tile wall. Water soaks through my clothes, fills my boots. I bang the wrist of the hand holding the razor against the tile to make her drop it.

"Who is she?" she screams. "Why did you fuck with me? Why—" Her voice breaks.

"She's my sister," I say, all my reasoning out the window now. "I shouldn't have fucked with you. I shouldn't have. It was wrong. I'm sorry, *malysh*."

"*Why* did you?" she croaks.

"I didn't plan on grabbing you last night, all right? I was just following you. Learning your habits. But you noticed me. And then those *mudaks* tried to rape you."

"*You* raped me!" She tries to head butt me again, but I move my head to the side. My nose feels slightly swollen and bruised from her earlier attack. "Why didn't you just... why did you?"

Her confusion guts me. "I'm sorry. You were tripping. I didn't want the drugs to enhance the trauma. So I waited."

She stares at me, soaking it in. "You didn't want... you were saving me from a bad trip?" Water droplets bead on her lashes. Her black eyeliner from last night has been washed clean, and she's even lovelier this way.

I nod.

"And Nadia is your sister?"

I ease back and let her slide to the shower floor now that the fight's gone out of her.

"*Da.* She's..." I stop myself. I don't want to tell Kateryna the details of what her father did. It's bad enough I will be taking him from her. I don't have to ruin her image of him, too.

"Your father ruined her." I leave it at that, backing away and closing the shower door.

Kat

I stand under the spray of water, trembling. Stunned by the new information revealed by my captor.

This is revenge for Nadia. His sister.

Whom my father ruined.

Ruined how? I squeeze my eyes shut. I don't think I want to know. Just like I don't want to know for certain what happened to my mother. Whether she's still out there somewhere or if my father ruined her, too.

I open the shower door and find Adrian's still at his

same post against the door. He's dripping wet, his clothing soaked through, his dark hair sticking flat to his forehead.

"Do you want to come in?" My throat is scratchy from screaming. "The water is still warm."

He shakes his head. "No. I shouldn't have mixed things for us. It was wrong. It only makes things harder."

I nod, suddenly deeply sad. It's probably just the let down from last night's ecstasy. My brain's chemicals have to be completely out of whack.

"Stay in there as long as you like. We have nowhere to be today."

Damn.

He's...kind. As I'd suspected last night, under the rough, grumpy exterior is a worthy man.

I keep the shower door open but back into the spray of water. I don't know if I'm trying to tempt him or just needing to stay connected. "Last night was a job?" I lift my hands to my hair, tracking Adrian's gaze when it falls to my lifted breasts. "You had sex with me to keep me from having a bad trip. That's all?"

"I didn't have sex with you."

"Yeah, keep telling yourself that. I had your dick in my mouth, and you had your tongue between my legs. That's pretty damn sexual."

He grasps the ends of the towel and pushes me against the wall. "I'm sorry, Kateryna. It was a mistake. It won't happen again."

He's saying the wrong thing. I don't want him to apologize and tell me it was a mistake. I want him to say it rocked his world the way it rocked mine. I want him to tell me he's the guy I thought he was last night. The sexy grumpy bear capable of everything, fulfilling all my deepest, darkest sexual fantasies. The guy who explicitly asked for and waited for consent but then took charge in the most deliciously dommy world.

And because I've had three years of therapy, I also recognize that I'm being childish and needy. I'm trying to attach myself emotionally to a guy who kidnapped me to use me for bait against my father. Believing that I'm somehow going to form a lasting emotional bond with this guy is stupid and foolish.

But then stupid and foolish are kind of my middle names.

"So it wasn't real?" I press. "You seduced me for my own good?" I let my disbelief show.

He turns stony, his dark glower returning. "For my own convenience," he snaps. "Get dressed."

I don't believe him. He's purposely putting distance between us. Part of me wants to get pissed–which is what he wants–and let him. The other part wants to keep pushing. Seduce him the way I did last night. Because we both know I was the one coming onto him, not the other way around.

"I need clean clothes," I assert. I got puke on my blouse this morning, and it smells now.

"You can wear my shirt," Adrian grumbles, nudging me out of the bathroom and into the small, darkened apartment.

I think about making a run for the door, but I'm naked, and I doubt I'd make it. I felt Adrian's muscles and show of strength last night. He's in excellent shape. He brings me to where a suitcase lies on the floor and opens it with his toe.

"Grab something," he orders.

I purposely drop my towel, holding his gaze for a moment before I slowly squat. The need to prove last night was more than convenience is strong.

Adrian's nostrils flare, and the muscles around his jaw tighten.

Good.

I hope he suffers. I hope his balls turn blue while he watches me.

I rummage through the suitcase, looking for something hard I can hit him over the head with.

He's onto me, though. "Take the one on the top," he barks. "Stop fucking around."

"This one?" I ask with mock innocence. I hook a finger in the neck of a soft, hunter green Henley and pick it up away from my body, so it hides nothing. "Do you have any panties for me?"

"Don't play seductress," Adrian says.

"I don't know what you mean."

"You must want punishment." Adrian's voice is silky and deep.

I smile because he's playing along. Either he's playing, or he's for real. I don't care which it is—I love this game. My nipples harden into tight beads.

Adrian's gaze dips to them, then he snatches his shirt from my hands and pulls it over my head like I'm a doll-baby he has to dress. He shakes his head like he's disgusted by me, but I know he's full of shit.

"No panties for you." He gives my ass a slap and captures both my wrists behind my back. My heart trips with excitement.

"Ooh, Spank me, Daddy."

"No. *Nyet.*" He propels me forward, back to the bed. There's genuine irritation in his voice now. I sort of love it. "I told you not to call me that."

"Sorry, Master," I say in a fake submissive voice.

He brings me to the side of the bed and pulls a fresh zip tie out of his pocket.

I fight him. "No more zip ties. Have you seen my wrists?" I demand.

He twists my wrists back in front of me and examines them. They are chafed and raw and even though his face doesn't change, I somehow am sure he feels bad about it.

He pins my wrists with one hand and uses the other to retrieve the gag he had around my head this morning. He twists this around my wrists twice, then wraps the zip tie on top.

"Not so tight!" I interject as he starts to tighten it.

He pauses, slows down. Measures carefully then lets it out a touch.

I make a show out of wincing and sucking in my breath like it really hurts. I mean, it does hurt–it's tender–but I'm definitely working it.

He backs it off another smidge. I keep an outward pressure on my wrists to hold them apart as he constrains them, and I don't twist or turn to show I still have a little room. When he finishes, he pushes me backward to sit on the bed. "Hands above you, *dietka*."

"No," I say stubbornly.

When he raises his brows with warning, I act petulant. "Why do they have to be over my head? It makes all the blood drain out of my hands. My shoulders and neck still ache." I roll onto my side in a fetal position, holding my wrists in front of me. "Here," I offer. "Find another place to attach me, so I can at least lie on my side."

Adrian drags in a measured breath like he's working to keep his patience, but as I suspected, the guy is a cinnamon roll under the tough guy act. He makes a daisy chain out of several zip ties and attaches one to the bed frame and one to my wrists.

When he stands, he peels off his wet shirt. The guy is gorgeous. On the wiry side and pale-skinned but built of solid muscle. When he turns away, I see he has a large, beautiful flame tattoo on his right shoulder blade with the Cyrillic letters that spell *mest'* beneath it.

"What does *mest'* mean?"

"*Vengeance.*" He turns and pins me with a brutal look, and my stomach flips.

"You burned someone in vengeance?"

He shakes his head, his lips turning down with bitterness. "Not yet."

A shudder of recognition runs through me. This is about my father, I'm sure of it.

"You're going to burn him?" I ask.

"Bratva tattoos are for crimes already complete," he says, shucking his wet jeans.

I wet my lips with my tongue, unable to resist asking, yet not sure I want to hear the answer. "What did you burn?"

This time when he meets my gaze, there's triumph flaming behind the dark promise of retribution. "I burned his factory down." He walks toward the bathroom in his boxer briefs but stops and turns when he gets to the doorway. "Don't make any sound," he says. There's a threat in his gaze.

"It's not like anyone could hear me anyway," I say, which is true because he still has the television turned up loud.

He disappears into the bathroom, and I hear the shower start.

Perfect. Time to make my getaway.

I twist and turn my wrists, pulling, pushing, wiggling.

Fuck.

It's tighter than I hoped, but there's still some room. I can do this. I can totally do this. It hurts, it's too tight, but I just might be able to get it over my thumb if I...

yes! I slip one hand out with a low moan of triumph. I'm free. I wrestle the other hand free and leap off the bed.

Where's my backpack purse? I grab it, digging through for my phone. The water in the shower shuts off. Eek! I need clothes. I keep rummaging for my phone as I race over to the door where I'd kicked my heels off last night. I stuff one foot in.

"Where do you think you're going?" A wet, angry Russian stalks toward me with a towel around his waist.

I freeze then throw open the door.

It's too late.

He slams it shut before I get through it and catches me by the throat. "You're in big trouble now." He holds me pinned against the door. My purse drops to the floor.

He's not out of breath like I am, nor does he seem particularly surprised or disappointed. I also note that he hasn't squeezed the fingers around my throat. Not enough to choke me, anyway.

Of course, he needs me alive.

Or does he? A chill runs through me as I realize that he's not holding me for ransom. Not really. He wants to kill my dad.

But this guy wouldn't kill me unless he had to. I'm sure about that.

At least…I think I am. He did give me his full name, which could indicate he doesn't plan to let me walk.

"Are you going to punish me, Daddy?" I taunt him, knowing he hates the name.

"Definitely."

I shiver at the way he says it with no hesitation. Like he'd already planned to, even before I tried to twist this into a sex game.

"I'm going to spank you until you cry, little girl."

Heat floods my pelvis, pouring down my inner thighs. I hate and love the threat at the same time.

I think about trying to knee him in the balls again, but he must read my mind because he spins me around to face the door and pins my hands to the door over my head. He pulls up the back of his shirt to bare my ass and smacks my ass on the right and left several times, hard.

My pussy clenches. It hurts, but it's also sexy to me.

He *is* playing my game. There's nothing harmful about the punishment. He's just using his hand. It may sting and smart a bit, but I seriously doubt it could make me cry.

"Were you running out with no panties, *dietka?*" He delivers another flurry of spanks to my ass, alternating one side then the other.

I push my ass out because he's definitely playing my game. He's talking about going out without panties, not about me trying to escape. Not about tricking him into not securing me tight enough.

I don't think he's even mad.

I let out a soft whimper but try to stay in place, stay still. I like this far too much. All the fear and adrenaline from trying to escape is now morphing into white-hot lust. Adrian doesn't hold back—not like he did last night. There's no stopping and rubbing in between.

It is quickly too much. Still not cry-worthy or anything but burning and dance-around worthy. I gasp, my pussy dripping honey as he sets my ass on fire.

I'm a little light-headed when he stops abruptly. He grips my wet hair and tugs my head back. "*Bad. Girl.*"

I almost come. So close. I felt a tremor, a twinge.

He holds me there like that for a moment, my wrists pinned on the door by one of his hands, my hair pulled back with the other. My nipples are hard, burning points against his loose soft shirt. My pulse hammers.

We're going to have sex now.

I hope he's as rough in bed as he is out of it.

I'll bet he is.

I tremble with excitement, with endorphins.

He pulls me away from the door and walks me back to the bed, still holding my wrists above my head and fisting my hair.

"Lie down," he barks, releasing me and giving me a shove.

I don't like that he let go of me. It feels wrong. But I climb on the bed, getting on my belly and spreading my legs, sort of wanting to keep the punish-y feel going.

Adrian zip ties my wrists together—way too tightly—and fastens them to the headboard, stretching me into a back-bend to keep them there.

I wince as I lean into them to get my knees under me and make myself more comfortable. Now my ass is out for him, ready.

And that's when he walks away.

5

Adrian

I can't do it. I know she wants me to satisfy her.

I definitely want to. My dick tents this towel so much it's a wonder it stayed on–the towel, not my dick. But fucking a girl who is bound and my prisoner isn't something I can bring myself to do.

If I did that, I'd be the same as Leon Poval and all his asshole clients and compatriots. I'd be the same as the horrible men who used and abused my sister while she was being held against her will as a sex slave in the basement of the sofa factory awaiting a long-term bidder.

And that thought makes me sick.

Even though it seems pretty consensual, even though I know Kat enjoyed her spanking, there's no way I'm fucking her.

"What in the hell are you doing, Russian?" she spits at me.

She's pissed, and I get it. I suppose I just did the equivalent of a cocktease to her. Left her blue-clitted or whatever.

"Don't you walk away. Are you taking pictures?" she screams.

I wasn't going to, but it's not a bad idea. "Your father will like this one," I say, finding my phone on the counter and holding it up. It really is a great shot with her reddened ass and the extremely degrading position.

"Don't you *dare*. Okay, then–" She flips her wet hair over her shoulder and ruins the photo by giving me a giant toothy smile. "Go ahead," she says without moving her lips. "What's wrong?"

She drops her hips to one side, contorting to roll to her back, where she opens her legs in a wide split and sticks her tongue out like she's posing for a porn shot. She sings some song about how she could be whatever color I like.

I shake my head. "Crazy fucking girl."

She sings more of the lyrics, pumping her hips and tossing her head about like she's in a music video, not tied to my bed.

"What is that? What are you doing?" There's something vaguely familiar about it, but I honestly don't know what's going on.

"Where have you been? It's "Grace Kelly," by Mika. You've seen the Grace Kelly challenge?" She sings some more of the song.

"What?"

She's doing crazy spread eagles and crisscrosses with her legs like a wild siren tempting me into the sea of blankets. "On Tiktok."

Tiktok. She's nuts.

I set the phone down and ignore her, going to the suitcase to find dry clothes to wear. I pull on a pair of boxer briefs, then my jeans.

She finishes the song then starts up again, except only repeating the one stanza over and over at different pitches.

It's maddening. Adorably bratty. I keep ignoring her.

Eventually she stops singing. She must realize I'm not coming back because she says, "I hate you, Adrian Turgenev. You are total shit. Seriously. I'm going to start screaming."

I turn and point a warning finger, not getting a chance to zip my jeans.

She glares at me and sucks in a lungful of air. She's giving me time to stop her. She wants me back over there. "Hel–"

I vault onto the bed and clap a hand over her mouth when she screams. My body's covering hers. She's naked from the waist down, the scent of her arousal tickling my senses.

There's both triumph and fear in her gaze.

The need to soothe her, to turn this into something sexual, to make it completely distinct from what my sister suffered makes me purr, "What's the matter? I get that pussy all hot and wet, and now it feels too empty?"

Her bright blue eyes lock onto mine. I see vulnerability and desire in them. It's the vulnerability that guts me.

"Listen to me." I ease back and slowly move my hand from her mouth. "I'm getting my knife. Don't move. Don't make a fucking sound."

She holds her breath, watching me retrieve my knife from my wet jeans and return to her. I cut the zip tie holding her to the bed. Her wrists are still clasped, but she can move around if she wants.

"If you want something from me, you come and get it. I'm not like your father. I don't take from women when they have no choice."

To make sure I'm not influencing her, I walk away, grabbing a pair of socks from my suitcase and sitting on a chair to put them on.

Kat watches me with a sulky glare.

I affect a natural stance. I'm ready if she tries to run for it, but I doubt she will. The sexual charge between us is electric. Intoxicating.

She flounces over to me. She has the air of a child who's been made to apologize for something they don't think they did wrong.

I make it easier for her, grabbing her around the waist and pulling her to sit on my lap, cupping her mons with my free hand. Her pussy is wet and swollen and my middle finger sinks inside her without me even seeking entrance.

"Is this what you need, *malysh?*"

She whimpers.

"*Say it.*" I sound like a dick, but it's important to me. The line between me and men like Poval seems thin and blurry. I've captured a girl against her will. I have her tied up and mostly naked. I need to prove to myself I'm not the exact same as the monster I'm trying to hunt.

I lightly trace around her clit with my finger, and she squirms, her head falling back on my shoulder.

"I need you to finish what you started." She still sounds petulant.

I hold her throat back against my shoulder, still rubbing between her legs with my other hand. "You want me to fuck you, *malyshka?*"

"*Tak.*" The syllable sounds close enough to the Russian *yes* that I understand her.

"I'll take care of you." I press my finger inside her again, pumping with a slow pulse. "How do you want it?"

She doesn't answer. I get it. She's obviously into being dominated. Giving me direction probably feels like topping from the bottom. I only know these terms because my buddy Pavel is into this shit.

"Hard and rough, Kateryna? Is that how you like it?"

She whimpers because I pick up the speed of my finger dipping in and out of her.

"Because I don't do gentle."

Not entirely true, but maybe with her it is.

"You want it on your knees or on your belly?" I haven't forgotten the way she offered herself up to me a few minutes ago. "Because you're definitely getting it from behind."

"Enough talk," she hisses through clenched teeth.

I pull my finger out and give her pussy a slap. "I decide what's enough."

She moans loudly.

I pull her knee open over mine and slap her pussy repeatedly, light and fast. "We'll make this simple. No fancy words. You tell me *stop;* otherwise, I do what I want. Yeah?"

She nods against my shoulder.

"Say it." I slap her pussy again.

"Yes!"

"Good girl." I lift her off my lap. "Go and get on the bed." I suppose it's one last test. I'm making sure she uses free will to put herself in position. That she really wants this.

She goes over to the bed and climbs onto her forearms and knees, her ass high in the air, making an appealing target. I walk over and run my palm lightly over her ass. It's red from the spanking I gave her against the door. Slightly heated to the touch.

I lift my palm and deliver another hard spank. She doesn't make a sound. "I don't like to hurt women, but I could definitely get used to spanking you," I tell her.

She says nothing but holds perfectly still.

"You are a very good girl, waiting for your fucking like this. You look so beautiful." I push my shirt up her back to reveal her breasts hanging down, and I pinch and roll the nipple of the one closest to me. "You have the nicest tits I've ever seen."

She lifts her head up, like she's surprised.

"Has no one told you that before?" I continue to pinch and squeeze her breast as I deliver another slap to her ass.

She hesitates, and I think she's not going to answer, but then she says, "No one I believed."

I don't like that, for some reason. It implies a lack of confidence, which I didn't suspect her of. From what I saw at the rave, she knows she's hot. She works it. She enjoys toying with men, trying to get something she seems to crave.

I fist her wet hair and squeeze, pulling it taut at the roots. "You believe me, Kateryna?"

She tries to look up at me, but with my hand in her hair, she can't, so I release her hair.

"Hmm?"

There's a pretty blush on her face like it pleases her to hear I'm in love with her rack. "I want to." I catch that vulnerability again, and it hurts my chest.

Fuck. She's going to get attached. I'm already far too entranced by her. And there's only one horrible way this relationship ends. With her father in a pool of his own blood and me holding the gun.

I don't mind wrecking my soul to get my vengeance. I don't care if I spend the rest of my life in prison or even if I die. But now it seems like I'm going to ruin this girl. And that was the one thing I was hoping not to do.

I didn't want her traumatized like Nadia. I didn't want her hurt.

But in my need to take care of her, to protect her from trauma, I've created a new weak point: her heart.

Not that her heart wasn't already bound to be broken

by losing her father, but to have it done at the hand of a man she's been intimate with—won't that completely destroy her?

But she's looking at me with those cornflower blue eyes. I can't pull back or stop now. I have to finish what I've started.

I grasp her shoulder and push it up to roll her backward. She rolls to her side, but I pick up her hips and prop her up on her knees again. "No," I say sharply, like she's displeased me. "You keep that ass in the air, so I can spank it." To emphasize my words, I give her three hard slaps. Then I push her top shoulder open again. "Now twist and give me that breast. I'm going to show you how much I like it."

I lower my head and suck her nipple into my mouth, then swirl my tongue around it and pull off. I grip it roughly and twist, but my words temper the action. "So pretty."

She lets out a shaky moan.

"Are you wet for me, Kateryna?" I ask. I haven't touched her pussy since she came to the bed.

"Yes," she warbles.

"Let me see." I climb around behind her and rub my fingers between her legs. Her honey coats my fingers, slick and sweet. I use it to circle her clit then dip my finger again and trail it over her asshole. "You want to get fucked here?"

"No," she says immediately, her anus squeezing beneath my finger.

"You might like it," I tell her and slap the place where ass meets thigh. I grab a pillow and shove it beneath her hips. "Lie flat, *malyshka*."

She slides forward to her belly and opens her thighs. I stroke again, putting my thumb over her anus as my two

71

fingers glide over her lubricated slit. It feels so dirty. So right. I give her ass another slap then murmur, "don't move."

I get a condom out of my wallet and return. She hasn't moved an inch. Kateryna is obedient as hell when she wants something.

"I'm putting on condom." My accent sounds thick.

"I have an IUD," she tells me.

I slap her ass. "You should still demand protection." I'm pissed off all over again about those *mudaks* who wanted to take advantage of her at the rave. Kateryna needs to raise her standards.

I take off my pants and shove down my boxer briefs, roll on the condom and position myself at her entrance. There's a voice nagging in the back of my head, trying to get control of me. It's telling me this is a mistake. This is the moment where I go too far. To a place I can't take back.

But I'm drunk on hormones now. I need Kateryna as badly as she needs me, and pulling back or pulling away has become an impossibility. I press into her slowly, easing in because I'm big, and she's tight. Inch by inch, I feed my cock into her until I'm fully seated.

I stroke her hair back from her face then fist and release it, giving her a firm scalp massage. "You good?"

She presses back against me. "Yes." She sounds breathless.

I ease back then slam in again. The pillow lifting her hips gives me a good angle. I can get deep inside her and hit her G-spot on the way.

"*Tak...tak*," she moans, apparently already on the way to satisfaction.

The pleasure is mutual. I haven't had a girlfriend since I left the Ukraine to find Nadia over a year ago. I've had a few hookups but nothing hot like this. Nothing so unapologetically kinky, so over-the-top sexy.

And Kateryna is by far the hottest girl I've been with.

I play with grabbing fistfuls of her hair and releasing it, sometimes tugging her head up to make her arch her back for a few strokes, then letting her back down to recover. I hold her nape down like she's pinned to the bed. I play with one nipple while bending her backward with a hair tug.

She's pliant. Enthusiastic. Every time I do something forceful or dominant, her pussy gushes for me. She apparently loves being mistreated.

I apparently enjoy being her abuser. The thought disturbs me, but I push it away. I can feel my own pleasure coming to a head. Surging forward to claim victory.

I ride Kat, slapping in harder and faster. I hook my hand in front of her neck to bow her backward while I fuck her. "You like it when I give it to you hard, *malyshka*? Hmm?"

"*Tak*," she cries.

"You take it like a good girl, don't you?"

She lets out a sobbing breath and squeezes my dick with her internal muscles. I can't hold back any longer. I rock into her with hard, forceful strokes, shaking the bed and making it bang against the wall.

"Yes!" Kat cries.

My vision turns hazy. The room swims and spins.

I give a shout and come, plunging deep inside her to fill the condom. She gives over in perfect tandem, her muscles milking my cum as she flutters and spasms her own release.

"That's it," I murmur, slowly rocking in and out to wring the last aftershocks from her. "Good girl."

∾

Kat

Good girl. Those words somehow both heal and wound me at the same time.

Maybe Delaney was right after all.

"Am I?" I ask, even though it's a terrible, needy thing to say. I'm going to freak him out just like I've freaked out every guy I ever thought was boyfriend potential. Because I'm not a good girl.

I'm bad.

Rotten to the core.

But Adrian pushes my hair back from my face. "Very good," he rumbles, a foreign warmth and approval in his voice making me turn my face to try to see his.

He drops a kiss on my temple. "You like to play bad girl, but you're nothing but good on the inside," he tells me.

I draw in a sudden terraced breath. I don't know why I feel like crying again. Am I going to cry every time this man makes me come? It's absurd.

Totally embarrassing.

Oh God, my eyes are already wet.

But Adrian doesn't make a big deal out of it. He doesn't freak out. He just thumbs a tear off the side of my nose.

"You're a strong girl, Kateryna," he tells me. He rolls us to our sides, keeping our bodies connected. He finds my clit with the pad of his finger and lightly circles it, wringing another small orgasm out of me.

I gasp and hold my breath then moan softly as I let it go.

"This quirk of yours–this fetish? It's your strength. Your flexibility is your strength. You won't break. No matter what happens."

He says the words fiercely, almost like he's willing it to

be true. Or programming me to be able to handle an impending disaster.

And I guess there is one.

Because he plans to kill my dad.

But I no longer doubt he will let me walk away. He's probably programming me now for our goodbye.

"After you kill my dad, you're going to let me go?" I have to ask.

He goes still behind me. "You're strong, Kat," he repeats. "You'll be all right no matter what happens."

I'm silent, turning over his words in my mind. I'd heard the goodbye in them, which drew my initial attention, but now I'm really thinking about what he said. That I have a fetish.

That it's a strength, not a weakness.

My father flew me across the continent to install me in a private English girls' school. All because one of his men caught me giving a boy a hand job behind our house. My father had called me a whore. Had raged and spat and cursed at me. *No daughter of mine is going to whore around like that. You will not be allowed back until you've proven you know how to behave.*

So I'd proven I knew how to misbehave.

I'd played the bad girl.

Now Adrian is telling me underneath it I'm really good?

Is that why it hurts so much when he calls me that?

Adrian eases out and rolls away. I roll to face him, hating myself for being so needy. He stands on the side of the bed, removing the condom, but he turns as if he senses my weakness. "You okay?"

I hold his gaze and nod.

"Hungry?"

I shake my head. "Sleepy," I say. It's true. As the post-orgasmic relaxation engulfs me, I feel like I could drift off to sleep.

"Me too." Adrian disposes of the condom and returns to the bed. He pulls the covers out and tucks me under then climbs in beside me.

The deliciousness of it washes over me. "Are we napping together?"

For the first time, I see the corners of Adrian's lips quirk. "*Da.* Come here." He arranges me on my side facing away from him, tucking his lower arm beneath my neck and wrapping the upper arm around my waist.

"Be good, Kateryna. I'm a light sleeper."

It's meant to be a warning, but for some reason, all it does is warm my heart. Maybe I'm still ridiculously celebrating the fact that we're cuddling. We're having an afternoon nap.

Yes, I know I'm being foolish. I know I'm in a terrible situation that is going to end horrifically. But I also believe whatever just happened between me and Adrian–whatever is still happening or is happening now–is real. It's true. He's not playing me. We shared a real moment, and we're having another one right now.

For the first time in my life, that sense of searching for something I can't quite find–that void that pottery started to fill–seems completely satisfied.

I found my center. I was somehow made whole again by degrading, rough sex, and a spanking.

Whole because it was acknowledged for what it was. It was an agreement. An arrangement.

A fetish, as Adrian called it.

I guess I have a fetish. And Adrian has it, too.

And he says it's the source of my strength. The thing I always thought was very much broken inside me might be my greatest source of power.

I'm not sure how that works, but I somehow feel it's true.

I snuggle my ass into the cradle of his hips, curve my back to meet his front. Adrian's breath blows warm across my nape. My eyes drift closed.

As absolutely batshit crazy as it sounds, I feel in my bones that this is where I'm meant to be. Right here in Adrian Turgenev's arms where I feel centered and strong.

6

Lucy

"Papa!" Benjamin shrieks, slapping his tiny hand against Ravil's closed office door.

"You want your daddy?" I ask, scooping him up, ready to distract him.

"He can come in," Ravil calls from the office. I open the door and set Benjamin down because he's kicking and thrashing to be free. He just learned to walk and can't get enough of it. He toddles toward Ravil in what looks like a drunken lurch, accelerating, then slowing when he navigates gravity to regain his balance.

Ravil's normally impassive face splits into a giant grin, and he holds his arms wide. "Come here, son," he says in Russian.

"Papa!" Benjamin repeats his first word, the one that lights up his father like a Christmas tree every time he says it.

My heart swells watching our tiny son arrive at the desk where Ravil snatches him up and tosses him in the air. To think I almost missed out on all this. I tried to keep our

78

child from his father. Didn't want him to know this man because he was in the bratva.

Every time I think of what a sad, stark existence Benjamin and I would be having right now if my plans had gone through, it makes me want to weep. I'm sure we wouldn't have thought it sad or stark because we wouldn't have known the difference. I would still be working my ass off at father's law firm, trying to prove myself to all the mansplainers there. Benjamin would have some nanny to watch him while I worked long hours, and I would've thought it was enough.

But having *enough* compared to having *everything* is, indeed, a bleak existence.

I just had to compromise on my moral high ground about the Russian *mafiya*. Had to realize that love is stronger than prejudice or trying to make things fit into that neat little package I'd thought my life was supposed to look like.

Ravil tosses Benjamin again and again, then snuggles him in for a big hug.

"How much longer will you be?" I ask.

"I'm finished." Ravil stands but rubs his brow—a tell that something's weighing on his mind.

He's the leader of the bratva and an alpha male, so getting him to even admit something's bothering him can be difficult, but it's worth a try.

"What's going on?"

Ravil sets our son down, and he promptly goes to the shelving unit and starts pulling all the books out. Toddlers are tiny hurricanes ripping through rooms and leaving total devastation in their wake.

I pull him away, but Ravil says, "Let him play. He won't hurt anything." He rubs his brow again. "Adrian won't take my calls."

Adrian is a newer member of Ravil's cell. The young man who brought us together when Ravil hired me to defend him.

"Do you think he's in trouble?"

"No. Not yet. He's communicating with Dima. I think he's dodging me because he knows his plan is unsound."

"He's gone rogue."

"Precisely, and if he fails, he could bring a shitstorm down on all of us. Not that I would have a problem taking Poval out myself. I just don't like getting blindsided."

"What is his plan—do you know?"

"More or less. If I tell you, you become an accessory."

"Attorney-client privilege," I shoot back. I represented Adrian the last time he went rogue going after the same man. The man responsible for bringing Russian sex slaves into this country and selling them at auction.

"He picked up Poval's daughter, who is a college student in England. He's holding her hostage."

Dismay flushes through me. "Oh God."

"You know Adrian." Ravil catches and holds my gaze to reassure me. "He won't hurt her."

I nod, drawing a breath to calm my racing heart. Wishing I hadn't asked. This is awful. But I cling to Ravil's words, which I'm sure are true—Adrian wouldn't hurt her.

"It's a bit ironic, isn't it? To kidnap a woman to punish someone for kidnapping women?" I manage.

"I know. I think that was his intention. He wants Poval to feel the way he did when Nadia was missing."

"Oh God." Now *I'm* rubbing my forehead.

"Yes. So I've been trying to reach him. Before he gets himself into a situation he deeply regrets."

"It might be too late for that."

"I know," Ravil says grimly. "And the trouble is, Poval might be enmeshed with the bratva—with other cells. So

Adrian could be stepping on toes in our own organization. I'll have his back, but there may be complications and consequences from this. So his not taking my calls is pissing me off."

Benjamin drags a book to Ravil and holds it out proudly. "Papa."

"*Spasibo*." Ravil's broad smile returns as he accepts the gift.

I melt, same as I do every time I watch this man with our son.

Catching my enamored smile, he reaches for me and tugs me onto his lap. "Ready to make another one?" He bites my breast through the emerald wrap-around dress I wore to work today. I'm in private practice now—only taking the cases that interest me since money isn't a concern and neither is the race to make partner at my former firm.

"No!" I laugh.

"When?" Ravil demands.

"Isn't one enough?" I'm getting older, which means future pregnancies could be harder.

"Is it?" he asks mildly.

I think about how Ravil would parent a daughter, and everything in me melts again. I'm still afraid that Ravil's past and sometimes still questionable present will bite us, but I know he's careful. Especially now that he has a family.

"Give me another six months," I say. "I need to wean this one first."

Ravil drags a hand up my inner thigh, drawing the hem of my dress up as he goes. "We'd better start practicing, then," he rumbles.

"Like we haven't been?" My laugh is husky.

Having a baby has been intense, but our sex life never

took a hit. We have tons of help. Valentina, our Russian nanny and housekeeper, is on deck every day, and there are plenty of adoring bratva uncles and aunts in the penthouse as well.

"We need to step it up," Ravil insists, his fingertips brushing across the gusset of my panties.

I rotate and straddle his waist. "You're right," I murmur against his lips. "The more practice, the better."

Adrian

I doze for an hour and a half, then get up, leaving Kat sleeping as I carefully secure her wrists to the bed without disturbing her.

When I check my phone, I see a text from Ravil: *Call me.*

I'm not going to. I can't. Still, I regret pissing off my *pakhan* this way.

I get dressed and head out to the drugstore to pick up a few things, including something to eat for our dinner.

I hadn't planned on entertaining at the place.

On my walk back, I return the call I got from Feodor, my local bratva contact.

"Feodor, it's Adrian," I tell him in Russian. "Everything set?"

"*Da.* They received the half-payment. Your place on the freight ship is confirmed. It docked last night. Tomorrow, all new cargo gets loaded."

"*Spasibo.* And the van and crate?"

"I'll drop them by tonight and leave the keys on the driver's side tire. Be at the dock by ten a.m. I'll text you the number of your shipping container. When you get there, ask for Rodion and bring enough in pounds for him to bribe the inspectors not to check your container. Get in it, and they'll load you up. Once the ship has sailed, they'll let you know when it's safe to come out, and they have a bunk room for you."

"Thank you, again."

"Bratva take care of bratva."

I thank him and end the call then go inside, where I find Kat in a semi-hysterical state, trying to rip her hands free. She's not screaming, though, which was my biggest fear. I left the television cranked, but I was worried she'd try to rouse a neighbor.

"Take it easy, *dietka*." I drop the bags on the counter and go to her, cutting the tie that holds her bound wrists to the bed.

"You *have* to take these off me," she huffs, her eyes wet with angry tears.

"I wish I could trust you, Kateryna, but I can't." I hold her wrists, hating how constricted and sore they look. "Come here. Are you hungry? I got some food for dinner."

I tug her to the half-kitchen to show her the food I picked up. It's crappy frozen shit, but it will do. I got some gourmet ice cream for afterward–hopefully she'll like that. "Which one do you want?"

She rummages through the bags with her bound hands and pulls out the bottle of hair conditioner I bought. When she turns to me, she looks so serious. "You bought conditioner for me."

"*Da.*"

"You bought... " She swallows. "That was very nice of you."

"Don't call me nice." I snatch it from her hands and set it on the counter. "I'm not that guy." She pulls out the box of condoms I bought, and her lips curve into a satisfied smile.

I take out the food options and wave a hand across them. "Which one do you want?"

She points to the packaged frozen pasta, and I tear off the plastic cover to put it in the microwave. "Ooh, Häagen-Dazs." She unveils the ice cream and inspects the carton. "Chocolate–my favorite."

I grunt, but inside I'm relieved I picked something she likes.

"May I take another shower?" she asks. "I mean, tonight? With the conditioner? Otherwise, my hair will get so snarled I'll have to cut it off."

I'm pretty sure she's fucking with me, but what do I know? I've never had long hair.

"Wait until the morning," I tell her. "I've had enough of wrestling you in the shower for one day."

"Yeah...I get that." She stands docilely in the kitchen wearing my shirt. There's something so doll-like and perfect about her. Those big blue eyes. The perfect bowtie lips. The way she presses and gives in and presses again. I have this weird fantasy about keeping her.

Wondering what it would be like to have her in the kitchen in my apartment, talking me into something she wanted. She's the kind of girl who could wrap you around her finger and make you move mountains just to see her smile. But she'd do it all with that yielding quality. She's not a ball-buster. She'd let you lead but offer plenty of colorful backtalk. Sulks and pouts and adorable tantrums.

If she were my girl, I'd probably give her anything she asked for. A steak dinner. A diamond ring. Someone's head on a platter.

But, of course, that fantasy ship won't ever sail. For one thing, Nadia lives in my apartment.

Nadia, my broken, ruined sister. The reason I'm here in the first place.

The reason there will never, ever be a future with me and Kateryna Poval in the same picture.

"Where did you learn English?" Kat asks as I take the food out of the microwave.

"America."

"Oh yeah? Where?" She watches me closely. I know she's trying to put things together.

I shouldn't tell her anything. I definitely know better. But I already gave her my name. I want her father to know it before he dies by my hand.

"Chicago."

"Oh really? My father lived there for a few years." She says it innocently, propping a slender hip against the refrigerator, but I know she's fishing.

"*Da.* he lived there until I burned his factory down and came for him in his own home. And then he ran."

Her lips part, eyes wide and alert.

Damn. I shouldn't have said that much to her. I don't need to make this worse for her than it already will be.

"I'm sorry," I say. "You didn't need to know that."

She shivers but lifts her chin. "I doubt he ran from you. My father runs from no man. He is far more ruthless than you are, trust me." She sounds slightly bitter, rather than proud, and something shifts around in my chest. An uncomfortable awareness that she might not be the crime lord princess I presumed her to be. Not spoiled like Sasha, Maxim's bride, who was the daughter of the Moscow *pakhan.* Perhaps she's suffered at her father's hand as well.

"Did he hurt you?" I ask, tension running through me like a deadly weapon.

I catch that vulnerability that makes me want to slay dragons for her. She swallows then shakes her head. "He is a cruel man. He didn't physically abuse me, but he's never shown me love. I seem to disappoint and disgust him."

"Then he's a fool."

I hate the man all over again. For a new reason now. Because Kateryna should never have been cast off or unappreciated. She's a sparkling gem of a young woman—bright and funny and full of life.

The microwave beeps, and I turn from her to open it and pull out her steaming food. I grab a fork to stir it up.

"You're right," I admit. "He didn't run from me. He left because the FBI was closing in on his operation. I guess I screwed up their investigation with my fire, which I regret."

Again, I'm telling her way too much. It's not like me to overshare anything at all. Not my feelings, not my plans, not details about my life. If things go south, she'll have all the information she needs to come after the Chicago Bratva. But something about Kat makes me want to lay it all at her feet. To offer these pieces to make up for what I'm doing to her. How I'm involving her. What it will mean.

I hold up the container of food. "You want to sit?"

She shakes her head. "Standing feels good. I've been in that bed all day."

I don't apologize. What would it do, anyway? Instead, I shrug and stay standing, too. I scoop a bite of the pasta and white sauce onto the fork and blow on it, bringing it to my lips to make sure it's not too hot before I hold it up to her mouth.

She lets me feed her, her gaze on my face. My dick gets hard when those pretty lips close around the fork. I can't tell if she's trying to be seductive or just can't help it. It's not just that watching her mouth makes me remember how incredible those lips looked stretched around my cock. There's something hot about feeding her. Knowing she can't eat except by my hand. My sweet, captive pet, captivating me with those bright blue eyes and her submission.

Maybe I'm as kinky as she is.

Yeah, I definitely am. Because now that I've had the taste of playing dominant, it's hard to imagine sex ever being satisfying without this dynamic.

Or is it just hard to imagine sex with another woman now? Like Kat broke the mold on sex partners for me.

"I know what you are," she says between bites.

I don't answer.

"Russian *mafiya*."

I offer another bite, still turned on by this simple act.

"I'm right, aren't I?" Some of her animation has returned. The performer side of Kat. Now I'm seeing glimpses of the girl who danced up on the boxes for attention.

"*Da*. The *bratva*."

"What does that mean? *Brotherhood*?"

"*Da*."

"And that's what these tattoos are for. They signify your crimes?"

"Crimes and the organization. The name of our cell."

"What is the name of it?"

I shouldn't tell her but for some reason, the words just come out. "Chicago Bratva."

She makes a scoffing sound. "That's not really a name. That's a geographical description."

"My *pakhan* doesn't have a flair for the dramatic. He keeps things simple."

"What is *pakhan*? The leader?"

"*Da*."

She chews slowly, shifting on her bare feet. I have to distract myself every time I look at her legs. Knowing she's bare under the hem of my shirt, remembering how it felt to be intimately acquainted with that sweetest part of her flesh, sends a fresh kick of lust straight to my dick.

Also, I don't have a foot fetish, but if I did, hers would be cum-worthy. They're dainty and cute, with perfectly painted toenails in Barbie pink.

"Did he send you here? To capture me?"

"No." I thumb a drip of pasta sauce from her lip and lick it. Her gaze tracks my movements, and I want to plunge my thumb into her mouth and see how hard she sucks it.

"So this isn't bratva business?"

I shake my head.

"This is personal. Because of your sister?"

"That's right."

"Wait, wait, wait." She holds up both her bound hands. "I thought Russian bratva members had to cut all ties to their family."

"That's true. That was supposed to happen. But my *pakhan* doesn't enforce that rule. Things are different in America, away from the old country's ways."

Again, I'm way oversharing. I need to shut up. To stop interacting with her. I'm losing my edge in so many ways. But then I lost my edge the moment I decided to grab her from the rave instead of sticking to my original plan.

At least by tomorrow, we'll be on the ship.

"You live in Chicago." She says it like a musing not a question. "For how long?"

"Enough questions, *dietka*." I feed her another bite.

"I want to go to America. The whole time my father was there, I begged him to let me visit, but he never did."

"He was protecting you." I don't like defending her father, but she seems hurt by it. "His operation in America was nasty. Nothing he'd want his little girl to be touched by."

88

She flicks her tongue out to lick some sauce off her lips, and it makes me want to kiss her senseless. Strange to think that I've been between her legs—*twice*—but haven't kissed that pretty mouth yet. But that's because we're not on a date. We're not even lovers, even though we've had sex. We're captor and his prisoner who happened to share a few interludes.

"No. He just doesn't like me much."

"That cannot be true," I tell her although the fact that she said it creates a wobble in my world. Not because I'm worried that Poval won't respond to my message about her. I know he will. But it bothers me that she believes that. "He paid a fortune for you to go to that private school you went to. And you can't tell me you ever want for anything. He's kept you sheltered and protected. He cares—that's just the way he shows it."

Jesus, now I'm really defending him. Definitely not a stance I want to take.

"He sent me here as punishment." She shakes her head when I offer another bite. "I'm finished, thank you."

She's thanking me for feeding her because I've immobilized her own hands. She's so damn sweet. I scoop the remaining pasta into my mouth in a few large spoonfuls.

"What was the punishment for?" I ask with my mouth full.

She watches me with a challenge in her gaze like she wants to see how I'll react. "For giving a boy a handjob when I was thirteen."

Maybe she thought I'd be shocked. I'm not. It's totally in character for her, and I have no judgement whatsoever about her hypersexualness now that I'm used to it. I just want to throat-punch any assholes who take advantage of her. She deserves to be treated like a goddamn princess, but I fear she's attracting the opposite.

I let my lips quirk slightly. "Of course you did."

She returns the smile, an uncharacteristic shyness stealing over her.

"Well, your father is a dick, so consider it a gift he deprived you of his nasty presence." I lift my chin toward the bed. "Go back to the bed, *dietka*."

"No. I'm sick of that bed."

"Sorry, *printsessa*. If I have to move you there myself, we'll go back to spread eagle."

She sticks her tongue out at me before she skitters away and does as she's told.

"Good girl." I heat up another frozen dinner for myself and eat it, keeping my eye on her.

She gets up from the bed to retrieve the remote control and starts scrolling through the channels on the television.

I log into the computer to check on messages from Dima and find his full instructions on how to send messages from my laptop from the ship to Leon Poval's phone, so they seem like they're coming from Kat's phone but are still untraceable.

Thank fuck for Dima.

Kat gets up and walks to the place where her purse is lying on the floor.

"Your phone is gone," I tell her. "I destroyed it."

"I don't want my phone. I need my lip gloss. And my gummies."

I follow her because she's close to the door, and I don't trust her. "I took the gummies, too," I tell her. "I'll give you some tomorrow."

She narrows her eyes. "What's happening tomorrow?" Smart girl.

"No questions, *dietka*."

She flips her hair and pads to the bathroom. I follow to make sure she doesn't take something to cut her zip tie in

90

there. I watch her pee and struggle with the toilet paper but don't help.

She makes a mess trying to wash her hands. If I weren't such a dick, I'd help her. I definitely wouldn't just watch because she's entertaining. Of course, she knows she's cute. She stands on her tiptoes and leans way over the sink, folding at the waist. My shirt rides up in the back, and I get a full view of that pert little ass, which she shifts from side to side as she tries to figure out how to turn on and off the water. She even hoists one knee up at one point, making sure I get a full flash of that soft pink flesh between her legs.

When she finishes she shakes the water off on me. "I'm bored."

Kat

Adrian scowls his grumpy face at me, but I can see the bulge in his pants. He liked the little show I put on for him.

I drop my bound wrists to rub the back of my thumbs along the ridge there. "If we're just killing time, maybe we could do it together?" I purr.

He catches my wrists and lifts them up, holding them between us. "I wish I could trust you, Kateryna."

"Well, you can't, but that doesn't mean we can't still enjoy ourselves."

That gets him. His eyes darken, and his cock firms even more behind his zipper. I'm not just a sex-crazed uni student. I'm just fighting with the weapon I know how to use best—my body.

That said, sexing up Adrian Turgenev is no hardship. He's hot and rough but also considerate in bed. Generous, even.

"Come on." I hook one of my fingers in his belt loop and pull him toward the bed. When we get there, I actually manage to work his button free with my thumbs before he takes over and unzips his pants for me. I drop to my knees to show him what I want.

He strokes my hair back from my face and sinks to sit on the edge of the bed, freeing his erection from his boxer briefs.

I go to town on his dick. Like my life depends on this blowjob–which is possible.

More likely, though, Adrian's life depends on it.

I mean, the more I think about this situation, the more I realize how likely it is to end with Adrian or my father dead.

But most likely Adrian.

He's one guy. My father has hundreds of men who work for him and millions of dollars to pay for more. Plus, my dad is ruthless. I've seen him kill a man with his bare hands. I know there's no chance my dad will show up to some meeting to get me alone. He's going to be ready to kill Adrian and anyone with him.

So even if I trusted Adrian completely and believed he wouldn't harm me–which I'm eighty percent sure I do–I have to escape. I have to divert his plan. Or talk him out of it. Something. I have to stop this train wreck from happening.

So I glue my eyes to the harsh lines of his beautiful face and take him as deep into my throat as I can, a little farther every time. I work on relaxing my gag reflex to get him deeper.

At first, his expression remains veiled. Stony, even. But as he starts to lose control, I see the real Adrian come out. He strokes my cheek with his thumb, cups my face.

"That's nice, *malyshka*," he murmurs. "So good."

I wrap my lips over my teeth and bob up and down over the head of his cock for a while then make him shudder but change the rhythm and take him deeply again. With my bound hands, I use the heels of my thumbs to massage his balls then work even further back, where the prostate gland supposedly lies.

"Good girl. So good."

There are those words again. The ones that get me wet and excited. Not that I wasn't already incredibly turned on by giving him pleasure. My nipples poke against his soft Henley, and I squirm my hips around, trying to get relief.

He plunges one hand into the open neck of the Henley and toys with my nipple. His touch is coaxing at first. A soft caress that turns rougher the closer he gets to coming. He cups the back of my head and pulls me on and off, forcing my head down and up.

I love it. If I didn't trust him, it would frighten me. The loss of control. Choking on his cock when he goes too deep. But there's something hot about it. Me on my knees with my hands bound. Him, forcing me into this.

I know he's not really forcing me, but we're walking an edge here.

"Kat...I'm going to come," he warns. He lets go of my head, I guess giving me the choice to come off.

I don't stop. I suck hard, even though my jaw aches from being open this long.

He shouts something in Russian and comes down my throat, and I swallow his salty essence down. It burns a little, but I love the taste. Love knowing I made him come. Love the way he touched me while I did.

"*Blyad'*, Kat."

I suck him clean, and he strokes my face.

"Good girl."

I sit back on my heels and look at him. "Do you always say that after a blowjob?"

"What?"

"Do you call them *good girl?*"

He shakes his head. "*Nyet*. Never. Only you."

"Because you know I like it?"

He shrugs.

I wait for more, but that's all he offers.

"Come here." He stands and tugs me up off my knees.

"Come where?"

Instead of answering, he leads me toward the kitchen area, where he grabs the conditioner he bought.

"Aw, do I get to shower?"

"I'll wash you," he says gruffly.

My pussy clenches and nipples tingle. Did he say...*he'll wash me?*

That's so...*hot*. And sweet. And definitely hot.

I let him lead me to the bathroom where he cuts the zip tie on my wrists and pulls his shirt off me.

"Go on." He lifts his chin toward the shower.

I turn on the water and wait until it heats as he takes off his clothes. He steps into the water, and I reach for him, eager to touch. Happy to have my wrists free. I stroke my palms over his muscled chest, making an approving hum as I touch.

He catches my wrists and examines them, stroking his thumbs over my pulse, bringing one to his lips to kiss away the bruises. "*Mne zhal'*."

It's close enough to the Ukranian *meni shkoda* that I recognize his apology.

"Let me go," I murmur to him, my fingers tracing the tattoo on his biceps.

His expression shutters, not that it was open to begin with. "*Mne zhal'*," he repeats.

"My father will kill you," I whisper. "How do you think your sister will feel then?"

His expression goes downright stony—and if I had to name the stone, it would be obsidian. Black obsidian. "He may kill me," he admits. "But I will take him with me."

Hot tears burn in my eyes. "Adrian, wouldn't it be better if you both just lived?" I raise my voice in frustration.

"*Nyet*. Not for all the girls—" He breaks off.

"What?" I whisper, knowing I won't want to hear what he's hiding from me. Is he protecting me? Or himself? "What girls?"

He shakes his head and takes my shoulders, pushing me back into the spray of water. "Tip your head back."

I obey. I know I'm not going to get any further with him. He's got some stubborn idea about revenge that he thinks he can't be talked out of.

But I will keep trying. I'll stay on the sister angle. What woman would want her brother to die to avenge her? I can't believe she would want that.

But then I forget all the silent arguments I'm composing in my head because Adrian moves to stand behind me, nudging me forward, out of the water's spray. After he pours shampoo on my hair, he starts a slow, sensual massage of my scalp.

I close my eyes and moan softly.

It feels so good. It's not quite as hot as I expected. More tender. Nurturing. It's an apology, I think. Adrian's sorry he has to involve me. Or believes he has to involve me.

I haven't had anyone take care of me like this in years. Maybe not since my mom left. My dad uses his money to maintain me, but it's not the same. It's not love. It's not kindness. It's not this.

He wraps a strong arm around my waist and gently moves me backward, under the spray of water again and fingers through my hair to rinse it.

Then we step out of the spray, and he applies the conditioner.

"More," I murmur because it's not enough. He adds more. My hair is a tangled mess, so I help him work it through to the ends. "Wait," I tell him when he tries to move me under the water again. "It takes a few minutes."

He grunts and picks up a bar of soap, which he rolls around in his palms. The slow lathering he gives me starts at my shoulders and travels down to each fingertip. Then down my back, up my belly to clean my breasts. He kneels on the tile to wash my legs down to my toes, then stands and gives my ass a great deal of attention. Around my buttocks. Between them. Down between my legs. He stands behind me and strokes my lady parts as his other hand kneads my breast.

"Okay," I whisper, not because I want him to stop, but because the water is starting to get cold.

I step under the shower and rinse off, and he joins me, stroking my long hair, smoothing his palms over my wet skin.

When the water goes cold, he shuts it off, and I turn to face him.

"You think I'm pretty," I say when his lids droop, gazing at me. I'm fishing for a compliment or confirmation of what I think is true. Being needy, as usual.

"Of course—you're beautiful." He cradles the back of my head and draws me right up against him, lifting my face to his. His lips hover over mine, soft and sensual, a contrast to the angular lines of his face. "Beauty isn't your power. It's not this hot little body."

I want him to stop. I don't like it. I wanted to hear what I wanted to hear. This wasn't it.

He touches my heart. "This is your power." And then he kisses me.

It's our first kiss, and it's a searing one. I loop my arms around his neck, lifting up on my toes to deepen it.

He catches my ass with his free hand, pulling me even tighter as his tongue sweeps between my lips.

I'm frantic in this kiss, craving it like I need my next breath. I twine my tongue around his, change angles, surge against him.

What did he mean was my power? My heart? My essence?

I'm confused by it, but I don't mind. Maybe I thought there would be a criticism that would hurt me. Like when Delaney asks me if there's meaning to my life beyond sex. But she *has* helped me seek satisfaction in other places like pottery.

"Do I seem like I need saving?" I pull away and ask. I'm breathless from the kiss, but I have to know. Does he see me as weak? Broken?

"Do I?" he asks me back.

I blink at him, bringing my fingers to his handsome face.

Yes. I don't say it out loud. Yes, he needs saving from my father. From himself. And I'm going to do it.

I'll be his savior.

He can be mine.

Because as much as I hate to admit it. As much as Delaney's been trying to get me to see that I don't need a savior or someone to take care of me or boss me around, that's exactly what I want.

I want a man who ties me up and feeds me like his pet.

Who both washes my hair and pulls it. Who wipes my tears even when he's the guy who makes me cry.

Maybe I'm deranged, but it's my kink. And Adrian fits the mold so perfectly it hurts.

And of course, I like the hurt.

"I'm ready," I murmur to him.

His brows knit. "Ready for what?"

"Ready for you to do depraved things to me."

His lips twitch, and he tweaks one of my nipples between his thumb and forefinger. He drops his gaze to his cock, which is hard and stiff between us. "Good. I'm ready, too."

7

Nadia

I work to calm my breath as we approach Rue's Lounge, the pub where Flynn and Story's band plays on Thursday nights.

Crowds aren't my thing. I avoid going places where someone might accidentally touch me. The worst, though, are nighttime crowds in places where people are drinking. Because the chances of getting touched skyrocket.

But I rode over with Maykl, the doorman at the Kremlin. He'll protect me from unwanted attention. He looks about as fierce as Oleg, Story's giant mute boyfriend with bulging muscles and crude tattoos covering his arms.

I know Adrian tasked him with keeping an eye on me while he's gone, and he's done a good job. I also know Adrian probably threatened to cut his balls off if he touched me. He doesn't even look me in the eye.

Honestly, while I feel safe with him, it's also uncomfortable.

But then, I'm uncomfortable with most people, so

that's not unusual. Even Adrian can make things worse for me.

It's like he's holding on to my trauma even more tightly than I am. I want to let it go, but it seems hard when he won't.

Hell, I know he's off somewhere right now trying to hunt down the man he believes is responsible for my four months of pure hell. As if killing one man would take away the evil in the world. As if it was just one man who tortured me. One man who touched me against my will.

It was so many of them.

But Adrian couldn't hunt down every one of them, so he went after the leader. A guy who probably doesn't even know of my existence. It's foolish, really. Probably dangerous.

We step inside, and I try to keep my gaze from zooming straight to the stage. Instead, I search the tables near the front of the stage where I know Oleg will have parked in advance, his bulky presence signaling to everyone his claim on the lead singer of The Storytellers. Our other neighbors from the building will gather there with him.

I find them right away–Nikolai and his girlfriend, Chelle, are sitting with Oleg along with Sasha and Maxim. Adrian's bratva brothers and their women.

I'm lucky he found such a tight-knit community. That they took me in despite my phobias and mistrust. Still, I don't feel like they're my friends. Like Adrian, they view me with pity. They remember my first months in the Kremlin when I screamed and clung to the elevator bar when Adrian tried to get me out of the building. They're careful with me. Sympathetic. Understanding.

Suffocating.

Finally, I let myself look to the stage. The music hasn't started yet, but the band members are setting up.

The microphone crackles and pops as Story's brother Flynn turns it on and bumps it against his lips. "Nadia's in the *howse*," he calls.

The little wings attached to my heart start to beat and flutter.

Flynn's wearing a light blue knit cap and a vintage Dead Kennedys t-shirt. I know it's vintage because I heard him telling a fangirl all about it the last time he wore it. It belonged to his dad, who was a popular local musician in the 80s.

I send a shy smile his way and wave, which makes the groupie girls who have also shown up early turn and stare with total hatred.

Flynn is the only person who doesn't assume I'm fragile. Who makes me forget how tiny and brittle my life has become. And also who makes me remember.

He's the reason I managed to get myself out of the building. Adrian had been trying for months and months to coax me out of the apartment and out of the building.

I'd left the apartment only to clean the building because Adrian's *pakhan* had offered me a job, and I wanted to contribute. I bumped into the beautiful, carefree Flynn leaving his band's rehearsal. He's everything I'm not–unburdened. Happy. Confident in a jocular, easy way. He invited me to come and hear the band play, and I found myself–impossibly–accepting the invitation. Suddenly willing to work on and improve my English. It had taken me several more weeks and aborted attempts to actually make it to the show, but I finally did. Now I'm rewarded every time with the golden boy's seeming delight to see me.

He doesn't know who I am or what happened to me.

He thinks I'm an ordinary girl who emigrated from Russia. And honestly, that's the biggest gift. I almost don't want to know him better because once he finds out my story, he will put the gloves on, like everyone else.

And just for now, I like to have one person who makes me feel normal.

Maykl and I take two seats at Oleg's table. I bob my head and smile shyly at everyone, avoiding eye contact and actual speaking.

"Nadia, you came out!" Sasha exclaims, throwing her arms wide. She's always larger-than-life exuberant, which makes me feel even smaller.

"I did."

Nikolai leans forward. "Any word from Adrian?" He keeps his expression casual, but I sense the tension behind it. Everyone's been asking about Adrian. They're worried, I think, but don't want me to know.

"I spoke with him this morning. He is fine."

"Did you let him know Ravil—"

"*Da.*" I bob my head. "I told him. He said he would call."

Nikolai frowns.

"Is he in trouble?"

The frown disappears. "Adrian?" He scoffs. "No. He can take care of himself. He'll be fine."

"Are you lying to me?" Being mentally unstable has advantages. One of them is being overly direct when I want to be.

Nikolai's girlfriend Chelle's gaze snaps to Nikolai's face to hear his answer.

He hesitates, and my heart starts to pound.

Maxim answers for him. "He's been known to make rash decisions in certain situations. We just want to be sure he has a chance to talk his plans through with me or

Ravil or someone with a level head who can help assess risk."

I fight to swallow and nod.

Rash decisions.

Risk.

My blood starts to pound in my temples, and I feel a bit lightheaded. Adrian's in trouble.

Oh God, what if something happens to him because of me? I wouldn't be able to go on.

Sasha elbows Maxim. "You worried her," she accuses. To me, she says, "The bratva has his back. Nothing will go wrong."

I'm trembling though. Feeling a little light-headed.

I probably should go.

Someone touches my shoulder, and I jump, ready to scream until I hear my name on his lips again. "Nadia."

Flynn's standing behind me, a dimpled grin on his face. There are two fangirls standing behind him, seeking his attention, but he's focused only on me.

I suck in a deep breath. I still feel dizzy but for a different reason now.

"Flynn."

He leans over and touches his cheek to mine for a side-kiss. The kind where your lips kiss air but your faces touch. "I'm glad you made it out."

For one hot second, the ground wobbles beneath my feet. He knows I have agoraphobia. But then I realize, he just means *out to the show.* Not *out of the building.*

"Of course," I say as if I have an active social life. "I love to hear you play."

"Hi, Flynn." One of the fangirls interrupts.

He ignores her. "Hey, there's a party afterward, if you want to hang out?"

"No," Maykl growls beside me, and I want to kill him,

even though I know I'd never be able to handle an after-party.

Flynn's brows pop, and he looks Maykl's way. "I'm sorry—are you guys together?" He holds his palms out. "I totally didn't mean to—"

"No," I say quickly. "He's just my ride."

"Well, I can ride you to the party."

"Nobody's riding her," Maykl snarls.

"Back off, muscles. It's a figure of speech." Even though Flynn is slender to Maykl's bulk, graceful where Maykl is jerky and hard, I suddenly believe Flynn wouldn't back down if it came to a fight over me. The sharp look of irritation he sends Maykl carries more aggression than I've seen from him before.

"Easy, boys," Maxim says smoothly, his relaxed posture remaining unchanged. To Maykl, he says, "Nadia's okay."

First time anyone's said that in a long time.

It's refreshing. Empowering, even. I toss my braid over my shoulder and give Flynn a genuine smile. "I can't tonight, but ask me again?"

"Yeah. Totally." He holds my gaze a moment with that pirate smile of his, and everything in me turns warm and sloshy.

"Flynn, where's the party?" The pain-in-the-ass girl behind him tries again. I want to tell her to fuck off, but even if I did, there'd be five more behind her.

And that's why even if I did learn to manage the agoraphobia, I can't ever get my hopes up over Flynn.

He's a total manwhore. A player. And the more popular The Storytellers get, the more groupies he has throwing their panties on the stage for him.

He's the definition of heartbreak.

He gives my shoulder a squeeze and winks before he

turns to address his harem, and I hide my blush by ducking down to rummage in my purse for my phone.

It's fine. Flynn is a fantasy, and that's the realm where he needs to stay. Getting any closer than we are would ruin it.

And right now, I need all the escapism I can get.

Adrian

I feed Kat another gummy and pull her panties on. I just made her orgasm twice—once with my tongue, once on my dick. She's completely blissed out, but I'm sick to my stomach.

I can't believe I'm doing the same thing those *mudaks* at the rave did to her. The same sordid shit that was done to Nadia. But it was the best way I could come up with for keeping her quiet while I get her on the ship.

I have a plan. It's a damn flimsy one, but it's the only one my conscience can accept. The one where I somehow make her halfway willing. And sadly, giving her the CBD gummies labeled for anxiety is part of that plan.

So is sex.

I move quickly, dressing Kat back in her tiny skirt, bra, and one of my t-shirts. She's floppy and compliant as a rag doll. Her hands are still free—I let her sleep with the zip ties off—but that's about to change.

"Okay, *malyshka*. It's time to move. I need to put your zip ties back on—just for a while."

"No," she pouts, but there's no fight behind the words. She's all floppy-sulky. I pick up her wrists and kiss them before I roll her to her side and fasten her hands behind her back. This is the most dangerous part of my plan. The part where many things could go wrong. I can't have her making any sound or getting free.

I fasten another zip tie around her ankles, and she gasps in exaggerated outrage. "What are you doing, Adrian?"

"I'm moving you," I explain again. "If you're good, I can cut these free when we get to our destination."

"I won't be good," she threatens.

A rush of fondness surges, and when it mingles with my guilt, I'm tempted to abort the whole mission. But no. I can't. I'm so damn close now. Besides, she knows everything about me. I stupidly, idiotically, gave her every detail, so her father could come after me and the Chicago Bratva. There's no stopping now. Not until he's dead.

"I know, *dietka.*" I stroke my thumb down the curve of her cheek. "But I can handle you."

That's what she likes. Being bad and getting gently punished. I'm using that kink against her— no, for her— fuck, I don't even know anymore.

I'm using her kink to try to make this work for her.

Bozhe moi, I hope it does. Traumatizing her would be unforgivable.

I leave her on the bed and wheel the large crate Feodor delivered with the van over to the side of the bed. I brought it in last night while she slept. At the same time, I scrubbed the place of all traces of our fingerprints or DNA.

Her eyes fly wide now, and she shakes her head. "No, no, no, no."

"It's okay, *malyshka.*" I scoop her wiggling, protesting form up and pivot to gently lay her in the soft bed of shredded paper inside the crate. "Here's what we're going to do. We're going to pretend I'm giving you a little cage time before your punishment."

She stills for a moment, her blue gaze wide. "What?" she croaks. Her nipples bead up beneath my white shirt.

I lightly brush my thumb across one. "It's a game, *dietka*. You've been a bad girl. I'm putting you in your cage to wait for your punishment."

"N-no." I can tell she's tweaked by the suggestion. Her eyes dilate, lips part.

I nod firmly. "I need you to be a good girl."

"No, Adrian." She's scared. Of course, she is. The gummies seem to take the edge of it, though. Her body remains relatively relaxed. "You can't do this."

"Please, Kateryna. I don't want to make threats or knock you out. Play this game with me."

She locks eyes on me, searching my face. "Where are we going?"

I shake my head and tie the gag around her mouth. "No!" she screams around it.

"Just until you're in the van." I tuck a sweater around her, so she won't get cold, close the lid of the crate, grab my packed duffel bag and quickly finish wiping the apartment of any prints or DNA either of us left behind before I wheel her out. Then I lock the door and leave the key under the mat for the landlord.

As soon as I get the crate loaded in the van–thank fuck for the liftgate–I open the lid to the crate and take off the gag, placing my finger on her lips. "See? You can trust me, no?"

Kat's startled gaze skitters around the ceiling of the van and back to my face.

"Be good." I leave her in the back with the lid off and shut the back gate then jog around to the driver's side. My phone rings, and I check the screen.

Ravil.

I decline the call, even though I know it will cost me when I see him again.

If I see him again.

I check under the front seat of the van and find Feodor left me a pistol as I asked. I tuck it in my jacket pocket now.

"Adrian?" The fearful pitch of Kat's voice makes my chest cold.

"Right here. I'll be with you the whole time. I'm not selling you. I'm not leaving you. Okay?"

"Cage time," she says weakly and relief rushes through me.

I was asking a lot for her to turn this into a sexual fantasy and not a terror, but she's trying.

Driving in the UK is a total pain in the ass because of the left-hand side of the road, but I handle it. I get to the dock, where I climb in the back of the van.

"Gag goes back on, *malyshka*. After your cage time, I'll give you everything you need. *Da?*"

She closes her eyes and hums softly like she's working to keep herself from freaking out.

"Good girl," I murmur and reattach the gag then close the lid.

I sure as hell hope this works.

I unload the crate from the van and wheel it in front of my shipping container. The guy named Rodion is there, waiting for me. I give him 200 pounds, and he opens it up and lets me in with the crate, closing it behind me.

I immediately remove the lid from the crate, so Kat can get eyes on me. "I'm still here," I say, as if my presence is a comfort to her. As if I'm not the guy who has her tied up in a crate about to set sail for America.

She tries to speak around the gag, but I hold my finger to her lips.

"Gag stays on a little longer." I stroke her face and lightly fondle her breasts, trying to make this pleasurable instead of frightening. It seems to work. After a few minutes, she makes a soft humming noise and lets her eyes drift closed.

I stroke my hand over her scantily clad ass, admiring her form with my palm. I keep her relaxed and calm this way for more than an hour when our shipping container is finally lifted and transported onto the freight ship.

Once there, I remove her gag. Her lids flutter open. "Where are we?" Her voice sounds hoarse. I fumble in my bag for a bottle of water and lift her to a sitting position to take a drink.

"Are we on a ship?"

"Yes."

Her eyes are wide and horrified. She looks around the inside of the shipping container. "Why?"

This is how my sister was transported to America.

I don't tell her that, though. My original idea of reenacting, or mostly pretending to reenact all the things done to Nadia now seems horrific. What was I thinking?

This whole plan is starting to feel half-baked. Is that the real reason I won't call Ravil back? Because I'm certain he'll tell me to abort-mission? That I'm out of my mind?

Fuck.

Now I'm not only out of my mind, but I've dragged Kat with me. Wild, sweet, beautiful Kat. The girl who is quickly becoming something precious to me.

Even though it's not safe yet, I pull out my knife and cut her wrists and ankles loose. "Come here, *malyshka.*" I reach in to lift her out. Instead of using my help to climb out, she clings to me like a koala bear, wrapping her slender legs around my waist and burying her face in my neck.

"I'm sorry, Kateryna. I know that sucked."

"It did," she agrees but doesn't sound all that upset.

I stand holding her, rocking from side to side like she's a baby needing comfort. After a moment, she says, "I do want to play cage with you, though."

A puff of laughter escapes my chest. "Good. Because we will have plenty of time to kill on this ship."

"Where are we going?"

"America."

"My father isn't in America."

My senses sharpen. "Where is he?"

"If I tell you, will you let me go?"

I only consider it for a moment. "*Nyet.*" It's impossible. I'd never get near him without her as my bait.

"Why not?" she sounds offended.

"I won't make you responsible for your father's demise. That isn't right."

"And this is?" She kicks her legs, and I put her down on her feet. She glares at me. "I think you have a contorted notion of right and wrong, Adrian."

Kat

The haunted quality in Adrian's expression tells me he agrees. His inner conflict is so palpable, I can practically touch it. I honestly don't know whether I surrendered to being put in a box because of the CBD gummies he gave me or because he practically begged me not to fight him.

The guy actually tried to seduce me into staying quiet.

He didn't try—he succeeded, I remind myself.

This experience is going to be ripe fodder for Dr. Delaney. We'll be picking apart my Stockholm Syndrome for years, I'm sure.

The truth is, I was turned on by the "cage-time" scenario. Adrian's got my number on that. That very fact alone would probably be reason enough for me to follow him onto a ship to America. Or jump off a cliff if he asked me to.

With him, I know satisfaction is possible. A resolution to the neediness that's consumed me since I was sent away from home.

At that moment, the metal container we're in bangs, and with a teeth-gnashing screech, the door swings open.

Adrian lunges for me, capturing me against his solid frame and covering my mouth with his hand.

A man stands in the doorway in a sweat-stained dirty shirt and a scruffy beard. He smells of stale alcohol–the kind that comes through the pores from the night before. He takes in the scene, his gaze lingering on my school-girl outfit and the way Adrian holds me captive, and it turns into a leer.

If I'd thought about recruiting help from him–which, for the record, I hadn't–it would've died the moment I saw that leer.

The guy speaks to Adrian in Russian–something about showing us our room–and Adrian grunts then propels me forward. We follow the guy onto the deck of a cargo ship. My stomach churns when I realize we're already far from shore.

So much for pottery. Or history. Or my first decent grade point average. Looks like I really am going to America.

By ship.

Adrian speaks to the crew member, who tosses another leering look over his shoulder and replies.

We're led down a flight of metal stairs to a small bunk

room with one bed. Adrian pulls me inside and shuts the door before he releases me.

"Is this my new prison?" I look around the small room. It's plain, but there's a round sea window with a built-in seat beneath it. I climb up and lean my back against the frame, looking out the window at the water. With a good book, this could be a sweet little nook. I can pretend I'm on a yacht.

"Yes." Adrian walks around the room exploring things. "Not bad," he says. "Could be worse. At least we have a window."

"Come up here with me," I invite. To my delight, he does, hopping up and leaning his back against the opposite side, his long legs tangling over mine

"What about my cage though?" I pretend to pout. "You said I get a reward and cage time." I'd been one part turned on, one part scared at the time. I can't believe I let him put me in that box and never freaked out. I guess the gummies helped.

It would be easy to demonize Adrian for this, but I see the good in him. He's trying hard to spare me from trauma. Maybe I'm being foolish and romantic, but part of me can't help but believe he's a hero trapped in a villain's role.

Of course, it's one he volunteered for.

Adrian sends me a feral grin. It's the first smile I've really seen on him, and it makes him look boyish and devastatingly handsome. "I plan to occupy myself with nothing other than using and abusing you for the next two weeks."

If he weren't smiling, I would take it a totally different way, but instead, his words light a white-hot flame of desire in my core.

He grips my calf and slides his hand up and down my

knee-high sock. For a moment, I pretend we're dating. He's my doting boyfriend, and this is our vacation on a cruise. The loving boyfriend I never had. Of course, I know nothing about Adrian Turgenev. Not what he does for a living nor the foods he likes. Not even his favorite TV show.

Adrian removes my shoes, tossing them one by one to the floor beside the single cot. He picks up my foot and starts massaging it.

"Feeling guilty?" I ask with a knowing smirk.

"Perhaps," he says.

"You should."

He accepts that as his due. "You deserve all the rewards now *malyshka*," he tells me. "You were a very good girl."

My breasts tighten at his words. Or maybe at his touch because the foot rub feels heavenly.

"What are the rewards?"

"Well, I'm not bad at giving foot rubs." He's working my foot with both hands now. He is actually amazing at it. But then I start wondering whose feet he rubs. Where he learned this talent. I want to murder every girl he ever seduced with that boyish smile and these firm thumbs working along the pads of my toes.

"Whose feet do you rub?" I ask, trying not to sound as jealous as I feel.

"I used to rub my mother's," he says. "She was sick with cancer, and it was something I could do for her."

"I'm sorry," I say. "Did…did she make it?"

"No."

"How old were you when she died?"

"I was fourteen. Nadia was just ten."

"How old are you now?" I ask.

"Twenty-six."

"What about your dad? Is he alive?"

Adrian gives a faint nod. "He's a drunk. He started drinking when my mom was sick. Now he's pretty much drunk all the time."

"I'm sorry."

He shrugs. "It is what it is."

"I was nine when my mom disappeared," I tell him.

Adrian frowns. "What do you mean *disappeared*?" His brows dip like he already knows the answer.

I shrug. "I like to think she ran away. But I don't know. There are many things I don't know about my father and what he's capable of."

I've never said it before out loud. Never voiced this horrific fear I have that he's the reason she left not only me but possibly the planet.

"Kataryna," Adrian says softly, his gaze filled with sympathy.

Tears pop into my eyes, and I quickly shake my head to send them away. "I know—*poor little rich girl*, right? Everyone assumes the crime lord's daughter is a pampered princess living a charmed life. But I'll tell you—it's fucking lonely. I don't have any friends in this world, Adrian, not even one."

What am I doing? I can't believe I'm throwing myself a pity party and inviting Adrian—a guy I would prefer to impress not embarrass myself with—along.

"That can't be," he asserts, his brown gaze intense, like he wants to make it true. Wants to convince me otherwise.

"It is true," I tell him. "Why do you think I'm out making random connections with sweaty boys at a rave? Falling for a guy who's holding me prisoner?"

Oops.

Oh my God, did I say that out loud?

I must be losing my mind.

Adrian stops breathing, his eyes wide and startled.

I wave a dismissive hand. "Kidding. I don't mean that."

A deep frown creases his face. "I'm here to use you. To hurt you, Kateryna."

I fold my arms protectively over my chest and hunch my shoulders. "Yeah. I know. But I'm a masochist, so I kind of like it. It's not a big deal."

Adrian's expression is nothing short of tortured. He stabs his fingers through his hair. "Yeah. I'm trying to make it a good hurt for you, Kat. But in the end…"

"In the end, someone has to die."

"Not you," he says quickly.

"I know." My nose burns, and I rub it to push the tears away, looking out the porthole at the spray of grey-blue water outside.

"If I live, Kat," Adrian begins.

I don't want to look at him because it hurts too much, but I end up doing it anyway.

"I–"

"What?" I croak.

"I mean, you wouldn't want or need this, but–"

"Just say it, Adrian."

"I will take care of you."

A strangled sound comes out of my throat, and I throw myself to the other side of the window seat, slamming my body into his. It's not a hug or an embrace, but I fall into him in a fetal position, hunched on my side against his chest.

His strong arms band around me, and he draws in a shaky breath. I feel his lips on the top of my head.

"I don't want you to," I say in a watery voice. It's both true and not true.

I'm actually horrified at how appealing his offer is to me. Do I really wish my father to be dead, so Adrian will have to take responsibility for me? Of course, he's only offering it out of guilt and responsibility. He wants me to know I wouldn't starve on the streets if he succeeds in his revenge.

He's not saying he'll marry me.

Be my sugar daddy.

Take me home. Well, maybe he would take me home. But I definitely should not be even remotely interested or excited by that prospect.

"Of course not," he says gruffly against my hair. "But if you did…"

"You make a good bad guy." I lift my wet face to peek at him and then tuck into his neck, where I kiss his skin. He smells of pine and leather. Strength and resolve. Kindness and courage.

"Maybe I'll kill you," I murmur against his skin, just because I think I should be fighting, and I know how absurd it is that I'm not.

He cradles the back of my head. I put my hair back in braids last night when it was wet, and he flicks one of the braids off my shoulder. "You probably will," he murmurs back.

8

Adrian

"I'm ready to send the text," I tell Dima. I had to call him while I had a cell signal.

Kat looks over at me from the window seat. I'm still in the bunkroom because I couldn't bring myself to tie her up again to leave it. Besides, I don't really have anything to hide from her now.

We're on the ship–she can't get off. She knows my plan.

"I was able to trace his last location. He was in Malta."

"Malta," I repeat, watching Kat's face.

I can tell by the way she stiffens that it's true.

Dima goes on, "I can't get any of his banking cracked, but I do have hers wide open. You could have him transfer money into her account, and I can transfer immediately out of it. Also, I might be able to trace it back to his."

"That works. You sure he can't trace it?"

"I'm good at what I do, Adrian."

"I know, I know."

"Did you call Ravil?"

"No."

"Are you planning on coming back, Adrian?" Dima asks quietly.

The wind goes out of me. I'm only about fifty percent sure I'll make it home to Chicago. To Nadia. But I haven't really felt the depth of what that means until this moment.

I scrub my hand across my jaw. "I want to," I tell him. "But I know the risks."

"Ravil and Maxim are expert strategists. Why wouldn't you run your plans by them?"

"I don't want to endanger the cell."

Dima makes a frustrated sound in his throat. "And if I refuse to continue helping you because you haven't made contact?"

"You know."

"You'd just do it on your own."

"Yes."

"You're a stubborn bastard."

I say nothing.

"Nadia doesn't need this, Adrian. She needs you here. If something happened to you, do you think she'd be able to go on?"

The familiar sensation of dread and rage grips my chest when I think of Nadia. Sometimes I'm not sure if she'll ever lead a normal life again. "*He* did that to her," I spit.

"Killing him won't change it."

My stomach roils, but I scoff. "Your woman has made you soft," I say. Dima moved in with a beautiful young Russian girl from our building last fall.

Dima hangs up on me, which I deserve.

It doesn't matter. He's already given me everything I need. I know he will continue to help me, whether I obey orders to check in with our *pakhan* or not.

Using the laptop, I compose and send a text message

from Kat's phone number to her "Papa". I include the graphic photos of her, along with the sardonic message in English, *Don't worry. I will treat her as well as you treat the women you enslave.*

He fires back a text immediately. It shows up on my laptop screen. *Hurt her and you will die.*

I send back, *Oops.*

What do you want?

I write back, *I want to cut off your dick and feed it to you. To watch you die slowly. To make your daughter suffer the way you made hundreds of women suffer.*

Finally. I have waited for this moment for so long. Dreamed of it. It's so fucking satisfying.

Who are you? Poval asks.

Even though I told Kat my name, it suddenly feels wrong to include Nadia in any of this. To say that I'm her brother. I don't want her sullied by the shit I'm doing in her name.

So I just say, *I represent all the women you've harmed.*

He shoots back, *Leave my daughter out of it. She has nothing to do with my business.*

Too late. Your daughter is now chained to my bed. If you want me to keep her alive, deposit $5M in her account within 48 hours.

When he doesn't reply immediately, I add, *I will return her to you personally when I'm finished using her.*

I shut the laptop and look at Kat. "It's done. Your father has been notified."

She turns her lips inside and looks away from me, out the window.

"I'm going to get us some food, *printsessa*." I grab a zip tie from my pocket. "Here." I loop it around her wrist, and she tries to punch me. I catch her hand and hold it still, then fasten another zip tie to the pipe running along the wall. "Just one hand. You can stay

119

right here and look outside. I'll be back in just a few minutes."

"What if I have to go to the bathroom?" she asks petulantly.

"Do you?"

"No. But I will soon."

"I'll take you when you do,"

"I want to punch your face," she tells me.

I catch her head and kiss her temple even though she just threatened to hurt me. "I know."

I explore the ship, finding the bathroom near our room, then taking the stairs up to the deck and walking along it.

It's cold on deck, the wind cutting through my shirt and chilling my skin, but I love the smell of salt air. I'm comfortable on ships–I grew up working on the docks in Vladivostok and then worked as a ship's engineer after I graduated.

That's part of why I chose to drag Kat across the ocean on a freight ship. Also because that was what was done to Nadia. Although now that reason seems irrelevant and weak.

I eventually find the kitchen and mess hall where five guys, including George, the crew member who let us out of the shipping container are eating from bowls. There's a large pot on the stove of what looks like Russian chili. There's also a half-empty bottle of vodka on the table, like they're already getting their evening drunk on.

"Ah, here is our stowaway," George says in Russian. "Adrian, was it?"

"Adrian, *da.*"

"I am Vladislav, the captain."

"Stepan."

"Lev."

"Grigor." They each introduce themselves.

"Where is the girl?" George asks.

I already had misgivings about this guy when he let us out. I didn't like the way he looked at Kat. Like she was a piece of meat. I don't know why I thought because these guys are Russian I could handle them, no problem. I didn't expect them to have my back, but I at least thought they'd be manageable. Icy tendrils of warning are seeping in, though. "She stays in our room."

Grigor, the biggest guy, grunts. "How much?"

"She's not for sale."

"I don't want to buy her. But how much for a turn?"

My hands clench into fists. Walls of anger close in on me. *Mudaks* like these used my sister. Fuck, maybe it was even on this very ship!

"Who are you saving her for?" George's eyes take on a curious glint. "Is she a virgin?"

It's a wonder I don't knock his teeth out right there. The guy likes unwilling virgins? He needs to die.

I want to tell them that she's not a sex slave except it would screw up my plan. If they suspected I had some prisoner I was ransoming, they might try to find out who is paying and get a piece of it. Or worse sell me out.

So I simply say, "She belongs to the boss. He wants her untouched."

"Who?" the captain asks, "Poval?"

My heart races. Holy fuck!

I can hardly function from the tumult of violence that overcomes me. The roaring in my ears. I choke on the bile rising in my throat. This must be the ship used to transport the slaves to America. The one Leon Poval used for his sex slave trade!

Two thoughts occur to me at once.

One: I can and will exact revenge on these assholes too.

But two: I'm in great danger here. Because if they somehow find out I have Poval's daughter, then my game is up, and I'm a dead man.

I consider telling them it's a different boss. Ravil or the Moscow *pakhan* Kuznets. But instead, I just grunt the affirmative and let them think it's Poval. Hopefully they're scared enough of him that they won't touch Kat. Now I just have to be very, very certain she doesn't get the chance to talk to any of them.

~

Kat

I TRIED to get free of the zip tie while Adrian was gone. Tried to reach his laptop where he apparently was able to text my father, to no avail.

He returns with two bowls of some kind of meat stew or chili and cuts me free. We sit in our window seat to eat.

The food is nasty, but we both finish. Adrian stacks my bowl on top of his and sets it beside him.

"Please tell me they have chocolate Häagan Dazs here."

A hint of a smile appears around Adrian's lips. "I wish," he says. "I doubt it. But I'll tell you what they *do* have."

"What?"

"Vodka. Lots of it. They were already half in the tank when I got our food."

"Tell me again why we're on a ship? And you now know we're going the wrong direction if you want to get to my father, right?"

Adrian's expression turns grumpy, and I think he's not

going to answer, but after a moment, he says, "I thought it was a mistake at first, too, but now I think fate led me to this ship."

"Why?"

He shakes his head. "Your father will come to me when I give him a meeting location."

"You want him on your own turf."

He studies me. "You're more worried for me than you are for your father, aren't you?"

I nod. "Yes. Not that you don't seem totally competent at killing someone." My gaze travels to the four green X's on his knuckles. "Were those kills?"

He doesn't answer, which I know means they are. "You think your father is invincible. That's normal for a daughter to believe."

"No, it's logical considering you're one guy with a very kind soul despite your villainous behavior, and my father has armies of assholes who have no souls whatsoever."

Adrian's expression turns sour, his upper lip curling. Now it's his turn to look out the porthole instead of at me.

"I'm sorry about your sister. About Nadia."

He shifts his gaze back to me, and I see a world of pain in his eyes. "I'm sorry about this. About using you this way. It was wrong."

"But you're still going ahead with it." I say it as a statement, rather than a question.

Adrian nods. "I can't turn back now."

"You *can*," I plead. "I won't tell. I won't tell my father who you are. I'll make up another story. I'll tell him I sent the pictures to shock him. You have the ones with me smiling, right?"

Adrian tunnels his fingers through his hair. "I'm sorry, *dietka*. I have to finish this."

I reach for his hand and interlace my fingers over the

tops of his. He stares at them, like he's confused by the gesture. "I don't want you to die."

He shakes his head. "I don't plan on it, Kat. But I'm willing. And that's probably what makes me bulletproof."

My eyes fill with tears. "Don't believe that."

He reaches for me and pulls me to his side of the window seat, settling me between his legs, leaning back against his wide chest. His arms wrap around me.

I breathe in his pine and leather scent. "Adrian?" I ask after a stretch of silence.

"*Da?*"

"If you did succeed…"

He goes still, listening. His breath feathers across my right ear.

"You offered to take care of me out of a sense of responsibility."

His lips find the shell of my ear, and he toys with it but doesn't answer. "Of course, I am responsible," he says after a stretch, and I want to crawl in a hole and die.

Of course, Adrian Turgenev doesn't want to keep me. It's absurd I would even hope such a thing.

"But…"

I hold my breath.

He kills me by not going on.

"But what?"

"But…if we'd just met….if we were both just strangers at that rave, and I took you home?"

My heart hammers in my chest so fast I think I'm going to pass out. "Yes?" I choke.

"I would never let you go."

My breath comes in on a sharp sob.

"Never," he repeats.

And then I'm crying. Real tears. I have no explanation

for why they're falling, but Adrian doesn't get upset about them.

He bends his knees up around me, so I'm cradled not just by his arms, but by his whole body, and he kisses the top of my head, gently rocking me like a baby.

"I would keep you, too," I tell him, dashing at the tears on my face.

"Only because I spanked you." There's laughter in his voice. Teasing.

It makes me laugh-weep even harder. "Yeah," I say. "That was fun."

"I'm going to do it again, *printsessa*."

"You are?" I pull his arms even tighter around me, like a security blanket I never want to let go of.

"Mmm hmm. You have a very spankable ass."

I tug his hand down between my legs, needing to feel something different than this ache in my chest.

He cups my mons possessively and bites my neck. "Does this hot little body need some attention from me?"

I squirm against his hand trying to get more friction. "Yes," I whimper.

He nudges me off the window ledge and drops down beside me. "Bend over the bed, little girl."

I do as I'm told, folding at the waist and putting my hands down on the small cot. Presenting my ass to him.

He gives it a gentle slap, and I wiggle for more. He slaps a few more times then flips my short skirt up and pulls my panties down to mid thigh. I'm instantly soaking wet.

"Is this what you need," Adrian asks. "You need this cute little ass spanked?"

I love how he always asks for consent, even as he's being masterful. It makes me feel safe.

"Yes," I affirm. I don't know why I need it. Delaney

125

would try to heal me of this sordid craving, but I don't want to be fixed. I absolutely love it. And Adrian does it just right. He is my hero even though he's dressed in villain's clothing. I want him to keep me. I want to be his little punished slave girl. Or whatever he wants me to be so long as he's doing his dominant thing.

He rubs my ass then grips it with both hands and plants a kiss on one cheek. "You're not too sore from earlier?"

I am a little sore, but I love feeling well-used by him. I love remembering how completely *owned* he made me feel. Not degraded—although I'm into that, too—just fully claimed.

"No," I say. "I want it."

"You want me to pound you with my big, hard cock?"

Ooh, he does dirty talk so well.

"Yes," I whimper, giving my ass another waggle.

He spanks me some more, warming my ass up with firm, stingy slaps. By the time I hear the crackle of the condom wrapper, I'm desperate for him.

I shimmy out of my panties and widen my stance.

"Beautiful girl," he murmurs, stroking a hand down my hip.

I register the soft-firm touch of his cock against my entrance, and I push back to take him.

"You going to take my cock like a good girl?" Despite the dommy words, he eases into me.

"Yes, sir."

He starts up a rhythm, slowly gaining in tempo. "On your knees," he orders in a guttural tone when it's time for a change. I climb onto the bed on my hands and knees, and he continues in that position, gathering my braids and tugging them back. "You like have your hair pulled?"

I don't like the actual feeling in my scalp, but I like him

controlling me. Like feeling a little forced, even though I know I'm safe with him.

"Yes," I pant.

He tugs a little harder, bringing my head back and forcing me to arch my back. "That's so pretty, *malyshka*," he says, and butterflies take flight in my belly. Pleasing him pleases me. "You're so wet, my Kit-Kat."

He remembered my nickname! I'd told it to him on the first night.

Also, he called me his.

Warmth wraps around me like a blanket. And then I'm too hot. Too needy.

"On your back," Adrian commands, in tune with my need for a change in position.

I roll to my back, even though missionary isn't my favorite position. Not to worry, he quickly makes it work for me by wrapping a large hand around my throat. He doesn't squeeze at all, just holds my throat, showing me he could choke me if he wanted.

His lids are heavy, lips are parted. He shoves into me with punctuated, hard thrusts that make sounds rocket from my throat. If he weren't holding onto my throat, he'd drive my body up, and my head would bump into the wall. I'm his captive. Literally and sexually.

Funny how I've never felt so free.

So unbuttoned. So met. Accepted. Bridged.

This man is my match.

If only I could keep him from getting himself killed.

I surrender completely to the sensations—the pleasure of Adrian moving inside me. The intensity of our position, the sight of his muscles straining in his chest and arms, the way his teeth clench around his ragged breath.

"Adrian," I moan, and his gaze snaps to my face,

almost in alarm. Like me calling his name during sex was the same as telling him I was falling for him.

But then he returns the intimacy. "Kat....Kat."

It's too much for me. A cry of pleasure echoes around our tiny room, and my internal muscles seize.

"Oh, fuck," Adrian mutters, going still for me, then pumping faster than ever until he reaches his own shouted climax. His fingers close around my throat–I don't think he even realizes, and I go with it, letting him squeeze out my breath. It brings on another equally strong orgasm, and I come and come beneath him, all over his cock.

"Oh shit, Kat." He releases my throat like it's a hot iron. "Baby. *Malyshka.* Kit-Kat." He strokes my neck. "Are you all right? I'm sorry."

My eyelids flutter open, and I give him a dreamy smile. "I'm good. I loved it."

"*Gospodi.*" He pulls out and drops beside me. "I thought I hurt you."

My smile widens. "You did."

His gaze turns fond, a smile playing on his lips. He kisses the bridge of my nose. "Beautiful, wild, funny girl. What will I do with you?" He backs off the bed, removing his condom and disposing of it.

"Keep me," I suggest.

Adrian

I arrange Kat on the cot with her head in the proper direction and lie down beside her.

Her words, *keep me,* bounce around in my head.

I want to keep her. To take her back to Chicago and fall madly in love with her while doing bad things to that hot little body of hers.

"Why were you living in England, Kat?"

"I already told you. My father sent me away."

"But after prep school. Was it your choice to stay in England?"

She rolls into me, resting her head on my shoulder, sliding her hand up my t-shirt to run her nails through the hair on my chest. "Yes."

"Why? You said you don't have friends there."

She doesn't answer, which makes me suspect there is an actual reason.

My heart thuds with an unpleasant notion. "Was it for a guy?"

Her light laughter relieves the jealous choke-hold on my throat. "No. I stayed for pottery."

"What?"

"My last year of prep school they got a new art teacher. She talked them into buying a pottery wheel and a kiln, and she taught us all how to throw pots. I fell in love."

"You love pottery." I don't know why I find that so satisfying. I guess I'm just happy that she has something. Something she loves. Something to work for. To believe in.

That's all any of us really need, isn't it?

For the past year, mine has been finding Nadia and then revenge. The ideas consumed me. Changed me. Made me into a hard, brutal man.

What if I'd found something so sweet and simple and perfect as pottery? Some art form that trained me into a meditative flow. Something that allowed me to get quiet without brooding. To make beauty with my hands instead of enact violence?

Maybe that's what Nadia needs to heal herself.

Kat lifts her head to look at me. "Are you laughing?"

"Never," I promise. "Why would I laugh? I love that for you."

She lets out a muffled giggle. "You do?" Her smile is so sweet and pretty it hurts. It makes me stupid and reckless. To think things I have no business thinking.

"Absolutely. It's the best thing I've heard in a long time. What do you like about it?"

She considers, nibbling on the inside of her lower lip. "In order to throw a pot, you have to really get centered. I mean, your thumb has to be centered in the clay, but that means you have to center, as well."

"Are we talking spiritually? Or Physically?"

She lights up, like she's pleased I asked. "Both. That's the thing!" She leans up on one hand and looks down at me. "I feel like I've been unbalanced my whole life. Like I don't know what center to orbit around. I was clay plopped on the wrong place on the wheel."

I brush my thumb over her nipple because her breasts are too beautiful to ignore, especially when one is in my face.

"And now you've found your center?"

"Well, no, not exactly. But I'm trying to figure it out. Clay showed me what I was missing–that I was off my axis. Why I always felt out of control and searching for something."

"So how do you center now, Kateryna?"

She draws in a breath. "I don't know. But I feel closest when I'm working with clay. Like getting it centered helps me to do the same."

I try to push back the desire to become her center. To provide the axis she orbits around. To never let her flounder or falter again. She needs to find that for herself. It's selfish and foolish to think I could ever be that for anyone. Still, I want to be it for her.

"If I got to keep you, Kateryna, I would build you an art studio," I murmur. "And I'd install a kiln right in the building for you. I wouldn't ever care that you were covered in clay dust every time I got you naked."

She traces her fingernail around my flat nipple, returning the favor. "You would?"

"Would it be enough?"

"Enough for what?"

"To keep you happy? Mean sex and a pottery studio."

She picks up the pillow beside my head and smacks my face with it. "We don't have mean sex." The goofy smile on her face makes my stomach squirm. She has moon eyes. Beautiful blue night sky against the moon eyes. "Yes. It would be enough."

She looks like she's in love.

I want her to be in love.

Which is horrible and cruel of me. Because I'm going to break her heart to savage pieces. Grind it to a pulp.

"What do you do, Adrian? When you're not out seeking revenge against my father?"

"I am engineer," I tell her. "I was trained as mechanical engineer and worked on a ship in Russia until my sister–" I look past her, swallowing the rest of my words.

"Tell me," she urges. "I should know. If you're going to kill my father over it, I should really know."

"No," I tell her. "You don't need to know. And I don't want to even try to justify my actions to you. You don't need to try to forgive me. Okay? You don't need to forgive it."

She blinks rapidly and swallows. "So, you're an engineer," she says softly, going back to the only part of the conversation that's palatable.

"I work as a structural engineer now. For construction projects." That was how Ravil put me to work remodeling his building floor by floor. I indulge in the fantasy for a moment. That Ravil gave me a space in the building to turn into Kat's pottery studio.

"I would only eat from pottery you made," I say aloud. "If I kept you. No other dishes."

She gives me the moon eyes again. "My stuff sucks. It's all irregular and too thick."

"I don't care. I would only eat off your plates."

She chuckles and traces one of my eyebrows with the pad of her index finger.

"I might—" I stop. Am I really going to say this? No. Once those words leave my mouth, I can't take them back. I can't tell her that there might be another way. That I might forego killing Leon Poval if I have enough proof and his location to send him to jail instead. Now that I know this ship was probably used to transport slaves to the U.S., I might be able to get something solid on him. And Ravil has a connection with the FBI now. A son of a bratva member. But it's such a long shot.

"What?"

I shake my head. "*Nyet*. Nothing."

"I think he killed my mother," she blurts.

Aw, fuck. She's trying to figure out how to forgive me. It can't be done. Shouldn't be done. She should hate me for the rest of her life. It's what I deserve.

"I know, *malyshka*."

Her eyes shine with tears. Her fingers flutter to her braids, and she twitches them nervously. "You know? Like, for sure?"

I shake my head. "I could tell you thought so. And… you're probably right. I'm so sorry."

She erupts into a hollow sob and drops her head down onto my chest. I pull her into my body and rub her back, holding her tightly.

How can I possibly consider going on? Tearing apart this girl who is already so broken?

This won't make Nadia whole.

All it does is dim another girl's light.

I kiss her head, my heart trampled and bleeding right along with hers.

9

Adrian

I wait until pre-dawn to go exploring on the ship. Judging by the loud voices that echoed into the night, the guys all drank themselves into a stupor. Hopefully, they're all passed out now.

When I brought Kat to use the restroom, that *mudak* George saw her out and taunted her. It made me want to bash his fucking head in although maybe it's for the best that Kat sees these guys are assholes. I don't want her thinking they might save her from me.

I head to the bridge, hoping to find it empty since we're out of port.

It is.

Using the light on my phone, I look around for the ship's logbooks. When I find them, I take pictures of every page going back four years. Then I photograph the port records going back as long, too. I need time to study them—to see if there's anything incriminating in them—particularly for Leon Poval.

Working quickly, I keep searching the captain's things, looking for any clues I can find.

The light of dawn seeps in, and I get an itchy urge to return to Kat. I don't want her to wake up alone. I don't like leaving her bound—especially with those *mudaks* down there nearby. If one of them found their way into our room, she'd be helpless against him.

The idea has me practically sprinting back, only to find everything quiet.

Kat stirs on the cot when I shut the door.

I cut her zip tie.

"What are you doing?" She sits up and stretches, looking out toward the porthole, which glows with the rosy light of sunrise. Her pale skin is flushed with sleep, making those blue eyes pop against her dark lashes.

"Everyone's asleep, do you want to go out on the deck for some fresh air?"

She rewards me with a brilliant smile, as if I've offered a day at the beach. "Totally." She climbs out of bed, dropping the covers.

I pick up the blankets and wrap them back around her. "It's freezing out there. Let's keep you warm."

She beams another achingly beautiful smile.

I can't help but let my lips curve up in response.

"Do I have to wear shoes?"

I look at her stocking feet, then turn to offer her my back, bending my knees. "Hop on."

I love how she does it immediately.

I carry her on my back up the stairs and out to the deck. The spray of ocean air hits our faces, and Kat inhales audibly then sighs. I bring her to the rail and swing her down to stand on my feet in front of me, looking out at the sea.

"Sunrise is my favorite," she says. Her voice is still husky from sleep.

"Yeah? Why?"

She shrugs. "It's like clay. Even if you totally screw up while throwing the pot, you can just ball it up and start over. That's what morning is."

I puzzle over that, but she goes on. "No matter what happened the day before, everything feels fresh and new in the morning. Like a do-over, you know?"

A do-over. That's what I need.

A chance to start over again with Kat. With this endeavor. Remold the clay.

How would I do it differently?

I probably should have called Ravil. Waited for more intel. Created a sounder plan.

"Before my mom left, mornings were our special time. My dad stayed up all night and slept until noon. My mom and I had the run of the house." She turns to look at me. "Like you and I have the run of the ship now."

God help me, I can't stop the thud of my heart against my chest. The need to kiss her senseless.

I indulge my desire, capturing her face in my hands and claiming those sweet, tender lips.

She kisses me back, looping her arms around my neck and hanging a little, as if her legs won't hold her up.

"Do you think they have any tea?" she asks when we break our lip lock.

"Hmm. I don't know. They seemed more like straight vodka types, but let's go see what we can find." I turn and offer her my back again. "Hop on, *malyshka.*"

She jumps on, and I carry her to the mess hall where things are…a disgusting mess still from last night. I find a couple mugs and wash them in the sink before filling them with water and putting them in the microwave.

Kat doesn't find any tea, but she does find packets of hot cocoa, which we empty into the heated water and stir around with a clean spoon.

I pull up a stool for her to perch on while I cook a few eggs in a pan. She sips her hot cocoa and watches me, still bundled up in the blankets from our bed.

Our bed.

I don't know when there became an *our* anything.

Maybe it was the moment we made it on the ship. After she let me put her in a crate and didn't even try to cut off my dick when I let her out.

Her trust in me changed everything.

It's becoming increasingly impossible for me to go on with my plan.

Tomorrow we have another port stop in Antwerp before we sail to America. I can use the phone and call Ravil. Talk through my options. Get a clear head about this situation.

I shove the eggs onto a plate and grab two forks. "Back to our room." I tip my head in the direction of the door.

"Back to prison?" she asks although there's no rancor. This surprising, crazy girl can't seem to hold a grudge against me for all the cruelty I've subjected her to.

"*Da.* Prison for you."

She hops off the stool and picks up both our hot cocoa mugs. The blankets trail on the floor as she walks ahead in her stocking feet. "Do I get mean sex?"

"Only if you're good."

Kat

Adrian paces our tiny room. It's late evening, and we've been cooped up here all day. The ship seems still. I think it dropped anchor. Adrian says they have one more port stop tomorrow before they sail across the ocean.

I'm staying alert. It could be my last chance to escape before Adrian brings this thing with my father to a head.

But he's seemed troubled all night—not that he's ever not troubled. My grumpy cinnamon roll. He's been checking his phone for service and cursing. I get the feeling he's rethinking his plan. Deciding if he's really going through with his vendetta.

I'd like to believe it's because of me.

Because he's fallen for me as hard as I've fallen for him.

If I got to keep you, Kateryna, I would build you an art studio.

He'd said it like it was a pipe dream. Something he didn't believe was actually possible.

Fear tugs at my solar plexus.

The voices of the crew ring through the halls. They're obviously drunk again—must be their nighttime ritual. I've thought about banging on the door and begging for help but quickly dismissed the notion. I don't know if any of them speak English or Ukrainian. I also don't find these guys to be particularly comforting.

But then again, if me getting out of this would save Adrian from his own suicide, maybe I should try it.

I hear one of them shout outside our door and then pound on it.

Adrian flies to our side of the door, leaning his shoulder there. He snarls something in return.

There's dark laughter from the other side and then shouts to his buddies. Their voices draw nearer.

Adrian shoots me a dark look, and I shiver because I see the killer in him.

"What do they want?" I ask.

"You," he says grimly.

My hand flutters to my throat where I work to swallow.

"Don't worry," he says. "I won't let them have you."

I feel like puking. What kind of men beat down the door of a woman, thinking they have some right to her?

Rapists, that's who.

Of course, they saw I was Adrian's prisoner. Maybe they thought...*gross*. Did they think I was some kind of sex slave? I've heard of such a thing in the news, but...

And that's when things click together in my head.

About Nadia.

My father.

Oh God.

Could it be something as sordid and awful as that? There's more pounding and shouts at the door.

No. I don't want to believe it. Yet all the pieces fit. I was having a hard time seeing my father being interested in someone's sister. I mean, maybe she's quite beautiful, I don't know, but my dad already has lots of women at his beck and call.

Oh... I almost wretch. What if all of them were...unwilling?

No, surely they would've asked me for help. He wouldn't bring that around me.

But maybe it's a business for him. I always suspected he was a drug dealer. Maybe it's actually...humans.

The door is locked, but apparently, they've found a key because Adrian watches the handle turn. He lunges for his bag–I'm guessing he has a weapon there, but it's too late.

They are inside the room.

I try to scream, but no sound comes out.

Adrian attacks, and he's good. He punches one, slams the door into another's head and kicks a third, but there are five of them and just one of him.

I dive for the bag, assuming he has something in there that would be of use, but the biggest, smelliest crew guy grabs me. His meaty forearm clamps across my windpipe, and he drags me to the door with a gleeful shout.

Adrian's still fighting hard, but he's on the ground. He grabs the legs out from the guy closest to him while he takes kicks to the ribs and gut.

"Adrian!" I choke.

When he sees me being dragged out the door, he bellows in rage, surging back to his feet only to get knocked down again.

The last thing I see before I'm carried off is Adrian's limp form being pulled across the floor.

10

Adrian

I spit blood down the front of myself when I regain consciousness. When I attempt to throw myself onto my feet I'm stopped by–*oh the fucking irony*–a goddamn zip tie around my wrists. It's one of my own–I'd left the baggie out on the floor, and it's attached to the metal frame of the bed.

"Kateryna!" I shout, yanking against it.

Where is she? Fuck, if they defile her before I get to her…

No. I won't let it happen. And I will kill every last one of those cocksuckers for trying.

I hear her scream in reply–she's in one of the other bunkrooms down here.

Fuck. Me.

"Don't touch her," I yell in Russian. "Leon Poval will have your head!"

Whether they believe I work for him or know that she's his daughter, I pray invoking his name will stop whatever is going on in there.

I wrestle with my zip tie, my muscles shaking with effort. I'm attached to the cot, but not the leg–I can't slip it off. I can't drag the bed, either. The damn thing is bolted to the wall, as things are on a ship.

My knife is right there in my back pocket, but I can't reach it. Why in the fuck didn't I use it on those *mudaks*?

I hear Kat's screams, and they clear my mind of all else but saving her. Gripping the rail of the bed I hoist my body into an inversion, lifting my hips above my head. I shake my legs and the knife falls out, except it lands on the floor, not the mattress as I'd hoped.

No matter.

Dropping back to my knees, I corral the knife between my two knees, then pinch them together and lift to pass it up to my wiggling fingers. I drop it twice, cursing and shaking with the effort, but I finally catch it in my fingers. It takes some work but I'm able to wrench it open and awkwardly turn it to saw off the zip tie.

Free!

"*Kateryna!*" I shout again. I would tell her I'm coming, but that would tip off the crew if they speak English.

She shrieks like someone hit her.

They *will* die. In the next sixty seconds.

I find the gun and ammo in my bag, load the pistol, and run toward the sound of Kat's screams.

I find two of the assholes crowded in the doorway, two more inside, and one trying to mount Kat on the bed as she fights like a little wild cat.

I aim and fire one shot almost point-blank.

Then another.

A third.

I don't get to fire the fourth because I'm attacked by George, who knocks me to the ground. The gun skitters across the floor. He punches me in the ear, gets an uppercut to my jaw before I manage to elbow him in the nose then flip our bodies, so I'm on top.

My vision bleeds red. I'm taking revenge, not just for Kat, but for Nadia and every other human being ever treated like property. Ever abused for someone else's amusement.

By now, the asshole who was on top of Kat has joined the fight, though. He wraps a meaty arm under my chin to choke off my air. It only turns me more ferocious. I use his grip on me, lifting both my feet to deliver a knockout blow to the guy beneath me.

I struggle, but I can't seem to get myself free of Grigor's hold. I twist and turn, throw elbows, and kick behind me to no avail. My vision starts to turn hazy around the edges then black. Stars dance before my eyes. The sound of Kat's sobs keeps me fighting. If I go down, she'll be alone with this guy. There's no way he wouldn't take out his rage at what I've done on her. I can't let that happen.

As my vision dims, the crack of metal hitting bone rings in my ears, and then I'm suddenly free falling to my knees. Gasping for breath. I stagger back to my feet to find Kat standing behind my assailant with a long-handled pipe wrench in her hands. She looks wild and vicious. Her lip is bleeding, and there's a red mark on her cheek that looks like it will bruise.

Grigor collapses to the side. I pick up the pistol and place a bullet in his head and another in George's.

"Kat," I croak, regret so deep I'm drowning in it.

It's unforgivable. I can't believe I did this to her. I want to punch my own face in. Shoot my own kneecaps.

But instead of hitting me with the wrench, she drops it and launches herself into my arms, her legs wrapping tightly around my waist, her arms strangling me.

"Kat," I choke again. I drop the pistol and hold her,

walking swiftly out of the room and away from the horrible scene. I don't want her to have to look at the mess I made of the crew. The faces of the men who tried to rape her.

"I'm so fucking sorry. So damn sorry." I carry her up to the deck to suck in the sea air. "I never should have let this happen to you."

She squeezes me even tighter. I can feel her shaking, and now I wish I hadn't brought her out here where it's cold. I carry her to the helm. "Adrian," she gasps. "Who's going to sail the ship?"

"Listen to me, Kat." I sit her down on the counter and clasp her head in my hands. "I'm going to get you off this ship. I just need to get a little closer to land, and then we'll take the tender to shore."

She nods her head. "Yeah. Okay."

Relief that she at least trusts me enough to get her out of this shitstorm hits me square in the chest. I don't deserve one speck of that trust, but I cling to it, anyway.

"Come here." I wrap her in my arms again. "Tell me you're okay. Please, tell me he didn't"

"No," she says. "I kicked him in the balls."

I cradle her face in my hands and press a kiss to her forehead. "Good girl."

"Adrian—" She blinks tears back. "What happened to Nadia?"

My own eyes sting, and for a moment, I can't speak at all. Then I simply nod.

Her lips tremble. "Is my dad a sex trafficker?"

My stomach's tied up in a knot. I wanted to keep this from her, to not taint her with the worst of it, but it's too late. I allowed her to be tainted by bringing her on this ship. Treating her like a slave.

I manage a jerky nod.

A tear spills down her cheek. "I hate him," she sobs.

I hold her and stroke the back of her head. "I'm so sorry. I should've left you out of it. I never should have let this happen. I'm so sorry, Kateryna."

"But she's safe now? Tell me, Adrian. I deserve to know."

I stroke my hands down her arms, and she presses her forehead to my chest. I don't want to tell her any of it. Some is too horrible to even speak of. But I would give Kat anything she asked of me right now, so I speak across the rust in my throat. "She was grabbed in a parking lot and taken to America on a freight ship. She spent four months in the basement of your father's sofa factory chained to a bed."

"The one you burned down."

"Yes."

"H-how did she get free?"

"I followed the trail to Chicago. I got a job with the bratva and used their connections to track down the operation. There were eight girls down there when I found them."

Kat's tears wet my shirt. She sits back and wipes them with her fingers. "If I were you, I would want revenge, too."

Funny, but my revenge—now that I've had a taste—feels so worthless now.

11

Kat

The wind is freezing, but I'm bundled in layers of blankets, huddled on the speedboat Adrian called the tender. The boat slices through the darkness, away from the freighter.

"What about the bodies?" I shout over the noise of the engine.

I know I'm in shock. I'm not clear on what my next five minutes look like, let alone my next days, but I do know I don't want Adrian to go to prison.

I don't want to go to jail, either, for that matter.

"I took care of it," Adrian says.

He cuts the engine before we reach the shore, so we coast in quietly. He helps me out of the blankets and onto the wooden dock, then tosses his duffel bag up. I'm wearing his leather jacket, like I did the first night we met. It smells of his clean, woodsy scent, and I don't want to ever take it off.

I could easily run. I'd have a head start and could probably lose him. But I don't want to leave Adrian now. I *can't* leave him.

Whatever happens, I have to see it through.

I watch as he wipes the steering wheel and surfaces on the boat down, cleaning it of our fingerprints. Then he climbs out without tying the boat, leaving it to drift off.

A huge explosion out on the water from the direction we came makes me gasp. I don't have to look at the satisfied gleam in Adrian's eye to know he was responsible. The evidence is now gone. His tracks covered.

"Let's find a hotel." He picks up the duffel bag.

I drag my gaze away from the fire on the water and nod. I let him lead. "Where are we?"

"Antwerp, Belgium. How's your Dutch?"

"Sorry, not a word."

"Me neither." He keeps one hand on my back as he pulls out his phone and checks the map app, then orders us a ride on Uber. Fifteen minutes later, we're safe and warm in the back of a car. Adrian rummages in his duffel, which he refused to put in the trunk of the car, and hands me my purse.

It's a simple gesture. Sort of worthless, since he said he already destroyed my phone, but it is comforting to me to have my own belongings in my possession. I pull out my lip gloss and rub it on my lips.

We pull up in front of the Radisson Blu Astrid, and I giggle a little. "Is this where we're staying?"

"*Da.*" He throws open the door, climbs out and holds his hand out for me to come his way. I follow instead of going out my own door because I like the attention. I like the care he's taking with me. And also because Adrian is a guy worth following.

I don't know whether his plans have changed, but I'm still holding out hope this can come out right.

Somehow.

When we get to the front desk of the hotel, Adrian presents them with a Russian passport and a fake name and pays with a matching credit card. "I'd like the best room available, please," he tells the clerk.

"Absolutely, sir." The guy's gaze slides to me and my soiled school-girl outfit. The braids. The platform heels. Adrian's jacket.

The guy thinks I'm a sex worker. I mean, who can blame him? It's five in the morning, and I'm dressed like a stripper who's been living on the street.

My stomach churns. What was fun for the rave has turned into something sick and disgusting now that I know about my dad and his business. About Adrian's sister and the other women.

Adrian draws me tightly against his side, claiming me like a treasured bride. He kisses my head as if to show we're a couple, not a business encounter.

The clerk averts his eyes and types on his computer. "How many nights, sir?"

"Three nights," Adrian says decisively, and I shoot a look at him that he doesn't return.

"I have a junior suite."

"I'll take it. Is room service available now?"

The clerk looks at his watch. "It starts in an hour." He slides two key cards across the counter. "Enjoy your stay."

"Thank you." Adrian hands me the keycards. Like returning my purse to me, it feels symbolic. He's giving me agency. Power.

I could open my mouth right now and tell this clerk I'm a prisoner, but Adrian risked it anyway. I could have told the Uber driver. I guess it means…I'm not his prisoner anymore.

Plans have changed.

I hope.

He picks up his bag and keeps his arm around me as we walk to the elevators.

"Are we staying three nights?" I ask.

"Probably not." Adrian shrugs. "But I wanted it to seem like we had an itinerary."

"What is your job in the bratva?" I ask as we step inside the elevator, thinking about how he took down five men, blew up a ship, and sent a boat adrift. Also that he has a fake passport and seems very good at this. It's foolish for me to be impressed, but I can't help it.

He's so damn capable.

And he's done all this to right the wrongs of my father. I knew he was a hero. An unconventional one, but still a hero.

"I'm the cleaner." He leans his back against the elevator wall and pulls me against his front.

"That makes sense."

"I don't usually make the messes, but when I do, I guess I go big." He shoots me a rueful look that makes my heart squeeze.

We get off at our floor, and I let us into the hotel room. It's clean and luxurious, and I head straight for the bathroom.

"Look at this tub!" I exclaim over the huge, deep soaking tub.

Adrian follows me in and turns the water on full blast, opening the bottle of bubble bath and soaking salts and dumping them in.

"Are you getting in?" I asked.

He starts unbuttoning my blouse. "You are," he says.

"Will you come in with me?" I ask as he slides my blouse off my arms.

Some emotion washes over his face. I can't quite identify it. Gratitude? Grief? Maybe a mixture of both. "You want me to?"

"Yes."

He unhooks my bra in the back, and I shake it off onto the floor beside my blouse.

"Whatever you need Kit-Kat," he murmurs, his warm palms sliding down my bare arms. "Whatever you want."

"It looks big enough for two." The bubbles are starting to form, piling higher and higher in the black marble tub.

I scoop a handful and bring them to my nose to breathe in the orange coriander scent.

Adrian unzips my skirt in the back and tugs it off along with my panties.

I rotate to face him and lift the hem of his shirt, pulling it up over his chiseled abs, up the broad planes of his beautiful hairy chest, and over the top of his head.

He starts to unbutton his pants, but I take over, wanting to undress him as he undressed me. Wanting to take a more active role this time. My fantasies are fun, but this time, it feels real. It feels like the first time Adrian and I have been intimate with each other. The real Adrian and the real me. Not some kinky sexual fantasy. We're not captor and prisoner. Not schoolgirl and teacher. Not master and slave.

"You are sexy with a gun," I tell him.

He lets out a puff of shocked laughter. "You're warped," he says.

It wounds me, and he sees it immediately, cupping my face. "I didn't mean that," he says. "I mean, I meant it in the most admiring way possible. I love your kink. I love that you're you. Wild and funny and free." He pulls the elastic off one of my braids and starts to unwind it. "You're beautiful– heartbreakingly beautiful. You're the most lovely girl I've ever seen in my life."

I suck in my breath, trembling. Not wanting to speak in case there's more.

"I wish–I wish things had been different. I wish I hadn't fucked this up." He unwinds the other braid.

I stroke *his* face now, wanting to comfort him. "Kiss me," I say.

He lowers his head infinitely slowly, his lips hovering just above mine, suspended in time. It's this captured moment–the space between our two bodies, both the magnetic pull and the resistance there at the same time.

And because I'm not the passive recipient this time, not the girl waiting to be acted upon, but the girl who makes her own choices and takes what she wants, I close the distance. I grip his face, pull it to mine and devour his lips. I slant my lips one way then the other, pulling his lower lip into my mouth. I sweep my tongue into his mouth and tangle and twine it with his.

He listens at first then responds with a fervor, snagging the back of my waist with his forearm and yanking me against his hard body. His other hand cups the side of my neck. My nipples tighten where they brush against his ribs. His cock thickens against my belly.

For once, I don't want the sex to be anonymous and hard from behind. The kind where I can stay in my head with the fantasy.

No, this time, I want it slow and gentle or maybe not gentle–scratch *gentle*. But I want it intimate. Looking into each other's eyes. Opening our hearts, minds, bodies, beings to each other.

This is love. This is what sex is for–this communion of two bodies. Two people. Two beings who are matched in a way no two other beings can be.

Adrian seems to want to take his time, too, because he doesn't spin me around and fold me over the side of the tub. Instead he gently pushes me away from him and breaks the kiss. "Let's get in." He tips his head in the direction of the water and holds my hand like a gentleman, helping me to step into the tub.

I stand in the center of it until he comes in too, then I sit and nest in the cradle of his legs, leaning back against his chest. His soapy hands slide all over my skin not really washing me, just touching.

He rubs circles around my nipples with his middle fingers. He cups my breasts and kneads them, then slides one hand up to wrap around my throat in the way that I love. I lean my head back on his shoulder trying to block out the events of the night. Trying not to ask what's going to happen tomorrow. Or later today, I guess, since it's already dawn.

His fingers slide down to circle my belly button then cup between my legs where my muscles catch and release.

I close my eyes and surrender to the sensations, let Adrian give me pleasure without desperately seeking a finish. He parts my folds and finds my clit, which he gently circles. Time stands still. With this touch–this undemanding, light touch, I am reborn. My body vibrates and hums with pleasure, releasing the ugliness of the night, coming firmly into the present.

Eventually the water cools, so Adrian lifts me to stand and follows me out of the tub. I hold a towel open for him, and he flashes me that rare, boyish grin before snatching it from me and wrapping me up in it. He captures me and pulls me back against his body. "Do you think I need to be taken care of, little one?"

"You had a rough night, too," I offer.

He rocks me back and forth in his arms, swaying like it's a slow dance. I don't want it to end even though I sense the ending is near.

Very, very near.

Adrian towels me off and leads me to the bed where he pulls the covers back for me.

"You're coming in, too, right?" I ask as I crawl onto the bed.

"Oh, I'm coming in." Adrian pounces, tackling me down on my back, his lips crashing down on mine. I lock my ankles behind his back, drawing his hips into the cradle of mine as I slide my tongue between his lips.

He braces his weight on his arms and lets me feel the warm tip of his cock. "I need to get a condom."

"I have an IUD," I remind him.

"I'm clean." He holds my gaze as he drags the head of his cock through my juices. When he presses forward, he moves slowly, like he's watching for trauma.

I use my legs to draw him in, rocking up to meet him.

There's something life-affirming and whole about the way our bodies fit together. The way they feel together. I need this as much as I need water and air. We hold each other's gazes as he rocks slowly in and out of me, dipping his mouth down every so often to meld our mouths with another searing kiss.

Like in the bath, there's no frenzy to finish. We're communing together, present and giving. His rhythm becomes my rhythm as we move in concert.

And then it's no longer enough. Adrian raises to his knees and lifts my pelvis into the air, holding me steady, so he can drive deep and fast. It feels like he could split me apart, and I want him to. I want to be consumed by him as I devour everything about this moment. This experience.

Our cries and shouts mingle, becoming more desperate as we both draw closer—still completely in tune with one another.

There's no need to speed up or slow down because we

both orgasm at the same exact moment—his roar of satisfaction carried by my higher pitched scream, the two sounds weaving together in a harmony all our own.

I shake and shudder around him, feeling the release all the way to my toes. "Adrian, Oh God," I chant.

He slowly lowers my hips back to the bed and nuzzles against my neck. "You don't have to call me God," he murmurs, laughter making his normally rough voice rich and velvety.

"You're the only one who makes me come like that."

"All right, I am a God, then," he jokes, rolling us to our sides. He strokes my hair back from my face, and we breathe together in silence.

"You should eat a little before you fall asleep," he says when my eyes drift closed. He eases out of me and gets up. "I'll call room service."

The sound of his deep voice on the phone falls like a lullaby all around me. A blanket I wrap myself in as I drift into dreamland.

Adrian

Kat doesn't stay awake to eat, which bothers the part of me that desperately needs to see to her well-being. I want to baby the crap out of this girl. Pamper her until she forgets every last horrible thing I subjected her to.

I wait until room service comes, then I eat and take the laptop into the living room and shut the door to the bedroom.

It's midnight in Chicago, but I send a text to Ravil anyway. *Are you up?*

A moment later, the laptop rings with a video call from

Dima. When the video comes into focus, I see Ravil, Maxim and Dima calling from Ravil's office.

"Adrian," Ravil says immediately. "I don't like when you dodge my calls."

"I'm sorry, *pakhan*. I fucked up."

He raises his brows at that admission. "What happened?"

Assuming he already knows everything about my plan from Dima, I start from what went down on the ship up until I blew it up.

"Where are you now?" Maxim asks. He's half-dressed in an unbuttoned shirt. Ravil probably roused him from his marital bed for the call.

"At the Radisson Blu Astrid in Antwerp."

He tips his head. "Interesting choice. You still have the girl, then."

"Kateryna," I say. She's no longer *the girl*. She's not Poval's daughter. She's my Kit-Kat. The lovely, wild, strong-fragile young woman I'm in love with. The one I have to let go.

"Yes. She's sleeping."

"Well, what are your thoughts, Adrian? I'm guessing you texted for a reason." Ravil is completely polite, but I know I'm still in the doghouse, rightfully so.

I don't answer. My mind has looped around and around. I'm out of plans and ideas. I just know my way didn't work. It's time to adjust.

"I'm...ready to abort."

Ravil lifts a cool brow.

Maxim smirks and leans back in his chair, folding his arms across his chest. "I knew that as soon as you said *Radisson Blu Astrid*."

I shrug. "Perhaps this is police matter."

"*A* police matter," Ravil corrects me. "That tactic might have worked better if you hadn't blown up the freighter."

"But you said you took photos of the log books?" Dima asks. "Send them to me. I might be able to trace them to his bank accounts." Dima flashes a grin. "I found them all. Oh, and the five mill appeared in her bank account. Did I tell you that? I can move it to one of our holding accounts."

My heart pounds. I could keep his money. That alone would be punishment enough for a man like Poval. Then again, it would give him a reason to come after me, and Kateryna knows everything. My name. Where I live. If she tells him, he'll come after the Chicago Bratva, and while Ravil can hold his own, I'm not going to put him into war.

"Hold off on that, please. Until I've figured out my next move."

Dima nods.

"A man like Poval probably would find a way out of prosecution, but it's worth a shot," Maxim says. "We've got our boy at the FBI. He could contact Interpol." Maxim scrubs a hand across his face. "Are you going to deliver him to Interpol, though?"

"Yes." I'd considered this. "I could get him here."

Or do I let the guy just walk free? I no longer care what's just or even about the justice Nadia deserves. I'm thinking about Kat.

What it would be like to have her only parent locked up.

Then again, it's not like he's really there for her anyway. She's been on her own, essentially, for years. It's a no wonder she's uncentered. Off her axis.

I remember my absurd fantasy about taking her home with me and building her a pottery studio, and my chest tightens painfully. In an alternate reality, I would live that life in a heartbeat.

He'll still be alive. He'll probably get off. And she'll have the five million dollars he transferred to her bank account. Which is good because his accounts might get frozen by proceedings. She would be all right.

I nod. "I will get him here."

"I'll contact Alex," Ravil says. The FBI agent who once wanted Ravil dead is now beholden to him. "No guarantees, though."

"I understand." I bow my head. "Either way, I'm cutting bait."

"Is she all right?" Ravil asks, somehow seeing into my heart with that laser gaze of his.

I frown. "No. I don't think so. But she's safe now. From me and those *mudaks* on the ship."

"She was always safe from you," Ravil points out.

I think of her bruised wrists from the zip ties. About putting her in the shipping crate. The near-rape I exposed her to on the ship. "No, she wasn't. But she is now." The best thing I can do for Kat now is to walk away.

As a good citizen, I will let the authorities know what I know about Poval. But that's the worst I'll do.

Anything more would be detrimental to my—no, not *my*. She doesn't belong to me. I have no claim on her whatsoever. Anything more would be detrimental to Kat.

"How is Nadia? Has anyone seen her?"

"Of course, we've seen her," Ravil says, pinning me with a hard look. "You think we wouldn't look out for her while you're away?"

I shake my head. "*Nyet.* No. Of course not. I didn't mean it that way. And I'm sorry I didn't call. I didn't want to drag your cell—our cell—into my mess."

"Your mess is our mess. We're brothers, Adrian," Maxim says.

"You cannot keep your mess from affecting us, which is why I don't appreciate you keeping me in the dark." Ravil's rebuke is mild, but my respect for him makes it hit me square in the chest.

I place my fist over my heart. "Forgive me."

After a pause, Maxim says, "Nadia seems to be doing fine. She came out with us to Rue's Lounge Thursday night. She might have a thing for Story's brother, Flynn."

I grind my teeth. I know it's true. I've seen the way she looks at him. And it's a big fucking problem as far as I'm concerned. That kid is a player, and Nadia's heart is already so fragile. There's no way I'm letting him anywhere near her.

"It's late here," Ravil says. "We'll be in touch. Answer your phone if I call, or I will superglue it to your ear when you return."

"I will—I'm sorry."

I end the call and send Dima the log book information then send a message to Kat's father.

Funds received. Kateryna unharmed. Pick up in Antwerp 10 pm CET tonight. Come in person, or you won't see her again. Text when you arrive.

Exhaustion rolls over me, but I push through, going down to the hotel gift shop I'd seen to buy Kat a shirt, sweater and a pair of leather boots. They didn't sell panties, but I bought her some fancy lotion, soap, shampoo and conditioner.

Then I return to the room and lie down beside her, curling my arm around her waist and pulling her against me. "Shh," I murmur against her nape when she startles. "Everything's all right, *malyshka*."

"Mmm. Adrian," she mumbles in her sleep like I'm a comfort to her, and my heart squeezes so hard I lose my breath.

Leaving her is going to fucking kill me.

12

Kat

I wake at two in the afternoon. I would've woken sooner–but every time I stirred, the comfort of Adrian's heavy arm draped around my side made me fall straight back to sleep.

God, I've never actually slept with a guy before him.

I've had sex–lots of it–from the moment I landed in England but never sleepovers. I couldn't while I was in the dormitory at school, and I've only had hookups since I've been living alone. No boyfriends. No one familiar in my bed, holding me like we belong together.

I find it delicious. I even liked it on the ship when we were sardined together on one tiny cot. I climb out of bed and pad into the bathroom. Adrian trails me—apparently, I'm still his prisoner. Either that, or he's decided there's nothing to hide between us anymore.

"Are you hungry?" he asks, leaning his shoulder in the doorway. "You must be famished."

I love this guy. I really do. I love the way he takes care of me. The way he thinks about my needs.

"Yeah," I admit. "I'm totally starving."

"I'll order room service. What sounds good?"

"A sandwich," I say. "And tea. I haven't had tea in days."

"I'll get you tea," he promises and backs away.

As soon as he's gone, I miss his presence. We've been in close quarters since Wednesday night. I'm beginning to feel like I can't breathe if he's not beside me. I use the toilet, brush my teeth and then climb in the shower. In it, I find all the things I could ask for. A fresh razor, big full bottles of shampoo and conditioner and a nice facial cleanser. Not the small hotel-size kind. No, Adrian had to have bought these.

I smile and shout, "Thank you for the conditioner!"

I hear the rumbles of Adrian's deep voice, but he's not talking to me. He must be on the phone to room service.

I take my time in the shower, thinking about making myself beautiful for Adrian. I shaved my legs, my armpits, and my bikini area. I wash my hair twice and condition it thoroughly. The whole time I sing "Grace Kelly" song by Mika. The one I'd used to try to make Adrian crazy back at his place. I sing it at my the top of my lungs. It's an invitation, and eventually, he takes me up on it. He pulls back the shower curtain with a smile on his face. "Did you say something about bending over?" he asks.

"You were listening!"

"I always listen *malyshka*." He shucks his clothes and steps into the shower with me.

"Are you going to bend me over and fuck me in the shower?" I ask hopefully, my hands sliding over his pects.

"Oh, I am definitely going to bend you over and fuck you in the shower," he promises, stepping close with dark intent. "I'm going to do all kinds of dirty things to you."

I lose my breath. "Like what?"

"Turn around," he orders.

I turn and face the wall, placing my hands on the tile like I'm under arrest.

He hooks his forearm under one of my knees, lifting it up and out to the side, so I'm standing on one leg, spread open for him. "I've needed to plow you in this position ever since you gave me a little show in my bathroom. Remember that?"

"I remember." I smile to myself.

"Is this what you wanted, then, *dietka?*" He positions himself at my entrance.

"Yes," I admit, turning to look over my shoulder at him. He's so handsome—so strong and sturdy. It's grounding just to be around him. To have his attention shining on me. Every indignity I've suffered since I met him has been worth it. I wouldn't trade even a minute of it. Maybe that's the maso in me talking, but I don't care.

I feel right when I'm with Adrian. Not so off-balance. So wobbly.

He makes me feel…centered.

If I got to keep you, Kateryna, I would build you an art studio.

I want to ask him what his plan is now. I sense something's changed in him. But I'm afraid of the answer. Afraid to lose this burgeoning hope in my chest. This fantasy that we might have a future. That he'll take me to Chicago and introduce me to his sister. Build me that art studio.

It's foolish, but I don't want to let it go.

Not yet.

Adrian pushes into me, bracing his free arm against the wall next to mine as he snaps his hips in and up. Already our bodies know each other. The rhythm comes easily. My body receptive to his, needy for his aggressive touch. The hot water in the shower has filled the room with steam, and I get dizzy from the heat building in my core.

I reach between my legs and grip the base of his cock, making a ring of my fingers for it to slide through as he arcs in and out of me.

His breath hitches, turns growly. He drills into me harder. Faster. "You're so hot, Kateryna. So sexy. I want to give you every orgasm you ever desired."

That simple expression is all it takes.

My intimate muscles spasm around his cock, catching and releasing as I come.

Adrian curses in Russian and pounds harder. I cry out in pleasure as lights dance before my eyes. I'm dizzy and off-balance, but it doesn't matter.

Adrian has me, and I know with all certainty he won't let me go.

He shouts, his movements growing jerky until he plunges deep, his dick pulsing as his hot cum fills me. I come again in the most satisfying climax of my life.

Adrian holds me up as we pant together then switches the water to cool until I regain my balance. I shut it off completely and step out, rushing to beat him to the towel. Laughing when he snatches it out of my hands and holds it open for me.

"Next you'll be holding doors for me," he teases, dropping a kiss on my forehead as he bundles me like pierogi in the towel.

A knock sounds on the door. "Stay here, *malyshka*," he tells me, wrapping another towel around his waist before he exits the bathroom. I hear him open the door and speak to the hotel employee bringing our food.

I only briefly wonder what would happen if I came out. Is Adrian no longer afraid of me asking for help? Does he know I wouldn't run from him now?

I wait until I hear the door close then come out and beeline—still naked—for the food.

Adrian's smile is indulgent as he steps into a fresh pair of boxer briefs. I envy him for having clean clothes to wear. "Keep running around naked, *dietka*, and you're going to get yourself fucked again."

I pull the silver covers off the plates. "Ooh. Darn. That would be a real hardship." I look over, biting my pinkie. "You're so bad at it and everything." The food looks so good I almost weep. I pick up a sandwich half and eat standing up, unable to even figure out how or where to sit first.

Adrian tugs on a long-sleeved shirt and slacks, then brings a handled shopping bag over to me. "I bought you some clothes." He pulls out an expensive-looking shirt and, instead of handing it to me, pulls it over my head.

I don't know why it makes me swoon, but it does. I like it when he takes care of me. I set the sandwich down long enough to poke my arms through the sleeves, and then he holds out a pair of leggings for me to step into.

"Where did you find these?" I ask, my mouth full.

"Downstairs."

"That was nice of you."

"It was necessary," he grunts. "Not nice."

"Whatever." I smirk into my sandwich.

"There's a sweater, too. You can wear my jacket when we go out."

"Where are we going?" I take another gigantic bite of sandwich.

I don't really expect him to answer because he never does, but he surprises me. "To buy you a coat."

Awww. We're going shopping together? Things really have changed.

Misgiving splinters off the sapling of hope I'm nurturing, but I ignore it. I don't want to question the future. The now is too beautiful to mar with it.

Adrian picks up the plates of food and arranges them at the table by the window, pulling out a chair for me. "Sit, Kit-Kat. I'll sit with you." He takes the opposite seat.

It's such a simple thing, but it makes me impossibly happy. I'm in my fantasy world— Adrian and I are a couple. This is what it would be like if we were traveling together. We'd stay at luxury hotels and order room service. We'd sit across the table from one another and make each other smile.

I wrap myself in this feeling. The warmth and rightness. The centeredness.

Some part of me knows it won't last, but I steadfastly ignore that niggling.

For this moment, I'm going to bask in the attention of the man I've fallen head over heels in love with.

Adrian

I can't do it.

I'm walking away from this endeavor entirely. No Interpol. No personal vengeance.

Kat deserves to be made whole, and bringing down or killing her only parent would just further throw her off-balance.

After we eat, I make quick work of tying up loose ends while she's in the bathroom brushing her hair and getting ready.

Then I take Kat out. I pretend it's for her–because she needs to get out after being imprisoned for four days–but really it's for me.

I'm savoring these last few hours with her.

I take her first to Meir Street to shop. We find her a beautiful red woolen coat, and I buy it for her, but she refuses to put it on.

"I don't want to take off your jacket." She hugs herself as if to keep me from removing it. "It smells like you, and it makes me feel safe."

My body liquifies into warm syrup.

"Oh." She blinks up at me, arrested. "Are you cold, though?" She's ridiculously cute.

"No." A lump crowds my throat. "I'm from Russia—this isn't cold to me. You keep it on, *malyshka.*"

After Meir Street, we head to the diamond district where I buy her a pink diamond stud to replace the little gold hoop she wears in her nose.

We sit down in a quaint restaurant for dinner. All the while, I memorize Kat's face. Her smile. Her exuberance that lights up and dims in a chaotic pattern.

I order coffee and dessert, then send a text from her phone—the one I put back together while she was in the bathroom. I set the phone down on the seat beside me.

"I have to step out to make a call. You stay here." It's an order but a mild one. She searches my face as I stand. I tap the table. "Don't leave, *malyshka.*"

"I won't," she promises, and I believe her.

That, more than anything, is what makes my chest fissure from the pain as I walk away, never to see Leon Poval's daughter again.

13

Kat

I sit in the window booth of the restaurant for a solid fifteen minutes before I get restless. I drank my coffee and ate the chocolate cake, and Adrian still hasn't returned.

It's rude.

I cling to my indignation for another ten minutes before the tendrils of misgiving creep in.

Adrian left me here.

No, no, he didn't. Surely not. He told me to stay.

Oh God! He totally left me!

A phone rings at our table, and I jump. I look under the table. In the shopping bag. Finally, I spot it in Adrian's seat.

I suck in a hard breath when I realize it's mine.

He left me my phone.

Maybe it's him!

I snatch up the phone and swipe before I see who's calling.

My dad.

"H-hello? Papa?"

"Kateryna," my dad snaps. "Are you all right?"

My eyes fill with tears although I'm not even sure what I'm crying over. "Yes." I don't sound convincing.

"Where are you? Put him on the phone."

I look around, as if expecting to find Adrian nearby, but of course, he's nowhere to be found.

He ghosted me.

Is this a trap? Is Adrian hiding somewhere nearby, so he can kill my father when he arrives?"

I can't even think straight. My mind is fuzzy, and a slow throbbing has started at my temples. Worst of all is a rising panic that makes my palms cold and clammy and my heart race.

"I-I'm not sure. Um…I'm staying at the Radisson Blu Astrid. Room 434. I'll meet you there." I end the call before he can answer and stand up from the table.

I need to get out of the restaurant before I start crying. I pick up the shopping bag and my purse and dig in it for a credit card as I stumble toward the door. I thrust it at our waiter when he hurries over.

"The gentleman already took care of the bill," he tells me smoothly. "He asked me to give you this."

He hands me a folded note, which I snatch and hold with trembling fingers as if it is my lifeline.

"Thank you. Thank you so much," I say breathlessly, rushing out of the restaurant.

Once outside, I gulp the cold air, trying to calm my racing heart. I open the note and stand under a streetlight to read it.

KAT,

I'm so sorry for the torture I put you through. It was

wrong of me to involve you, and I will regret how I treated you until the day I die.

I don't expect your forgiveness, but I want you to know that for you, I have halted my vendetta against your father. You changed me, and you changed my heart.

You know my name and where I live. Do what you need to do.

I will think of you throwing pots. Finding your center. Being bright, beautiful you.

You took my heart, and I don't want it back.

–A

"ADRIAN," I whisper, pressing the note to my chest as tears stream down my cheeks. "You left me."

I now know Delaney was right–I have abandonment issues.

Because I really shouldn't feel like my limbs have just been torn from my body. Nothing–*nothing*–has ever hurt so badly as this.

I know the note was full of love. It was an apology and an honoring. But I want none of it.

I just want Adrian back.

Damn him! How could he do this to me? Could he really think him leaving me was a gift?

I suppose the gift is my father living. And Adrian couldn't very well stick around with my father still living.

My stomach churns wondering what I'm going to do about my dad.

Do what you need to do.

As if. There's no way I'm going to give up Adrian's identity to my homicidal father.

My homicidal, sex-trafficking father.

Ugh. I don't even want to return to the hotel. I don't know how I'll look my dad in the eye again without wanting to puke. I find a bench to sit on, so I can gather myself and think. I need to get a taxi or Uber. I need to get my story straight.

I unlock my phone to order a car, and I see the text messages are open. A whole thread between Adrian and my dad. The photos of me. His demands. My father's replies.

I read through them.

The money went into my account? I open my bank app to check the balance and suck in my breath.

Almost four million pounds.

It's still there. Adrian didn't take it. He should have—it will be harder for me to make up a story about my captor when...

Wait.

I re-read the texts. A giddy-sick feeling comes over me as I consider my latest idea.

Yes...it could work. My dad will blow a gasket, but it's better than him chasing down Adrian.

I open the Uber app and order a car.

I can do this. I suck in a shaky breath, hold it and let it out slowly to the count of ten, the way Delaney taught me.

I can totally do this.

Adrian

"I need the first flight to Chicago?"

I'm at the airport. After leaving Kat in the restaurant, I swung back to pick up my duffel from the hotel then headed straight here. There's a hole in my heart the size of a tree trunk, and distance seems the best solution.

Besides, Leon Poval is probably already scouring the

city for me. Funny how a week ago that would've been the best possible news. But now that I've resolved to leaving him untouched, it's a big problem.

A worse problem will be if he shows up in Chicago. But I'll deal with that when it happens.

Correction—we'll deal with that. The bratva will have my back. And I wouldn't cry too hard if one of them had to take Poval out since I couldn't in good conscience do it.

"The first flight we have is tomorrow at 8 a.m."

Damn. I was hoping for some kind of red eye leaving tonight. "I'll take it." I hand over a different passport and credit card than I used at the hotel and take the tickets. I consider staying the night at the airport, but it seems like it might attract attention, so I leave, taking a taxi to the closest hotel.

I get there and toss the duffel bag on the bed and walk in a circle with my hands on my head. I don't want to be here. The hotel room reminds me of Kat. Everything reminds me of Kat.

I should've stayed at the airport. I deserve the discomfort of sleeping upright in an airport lounger.

I pace around the small room, making laps until I run into a wall and bang my forehead on it.

Fuck!

I did the right thing. I know I did. I should feel better than I do.

I don't even care about my revenge. I don't feel like I let Nadia down although I have. Except I know now that it wasn't for her. She didn't need me to do this. I may have told myself that story, but it wasn't true. I came on this fucked-up journey for myself. *I* felt violated by Poval on behalf of my sister, and *I* was the one who wanted revenge.

It was a stupid, glorified alpha male endeavor that doesn't fix or right anything for Nadia.

All I did was hurt Kat.

But she got the last laugh.

Because right now, it feels like a grenade went off in the center of my chest, leaving the whole cavity gaping open. Torn. Bleeding. And most of all, empty.

I let myself indulge a little fantasy about seeing Kat again. Maybe I'd go to Liverpool. I wouldn't let her see me–I'd do a better job tailing her this time. But I'd just get to see her. To be near her. To know she's okay. Maybe to step in if anyone fucked with her again.

Gospodi, that's stupid.

Of course, I'm not going to Liverpool.

I can't ever see Kat again, and that's the part that fucking kills me.

Ravil calls, and I pick up.

"You actually answered my call." He's going to keep busting my balls for a while on this one. "Interpol wants Poval's location," he tells me. "I just texted you the phone number of who you should contact. He's wanted in Ukraine, Italy, and Romania. Also, the U.S. would file extradition papers to bring him over here for charges of sex trafficking."

"I'm letting him go."

Ravil's silent for a moment. I wait for him to rip me a new one about the danger I put our cell in over the way I handled this, but all he says is, "Your decision."

"Thank you. I made it."

"If you change your mind, Interpol knows he's in Antwerp and are awaiting your call."

"I won't change my mind."

"All right. What do you need from us, Adrian?"

"I let Kateryna go. I'm coming home on the first flight out in the morning."

"We'll see you tomorrow, then."

"Yeah. *Da skorava.*" I end the call.

The heaviness in the pit of my stomach hasn't lessened one bit.

The thought of returning home—or to what has become home—should be a relief. Nadia needs me. I will be with my bratva brothers. But I can't even picture myself there.

I've changed so much in the past four days. Kat changed me. And I don't even know how I'll make it through one day without her.

Kat

In the Uber on the way to the hotel, I take off Adrian's leather jacket and lift it to my face to breathe in his scent. At least I have this one thing of his to remember him by.

I stuff it in the shopping bag and put on the new one before I get out.

In the hotel, I find the door to our hotel room ajar and the room filled with men. Six pistols swing and point at me.

I drop the shopping bag and lift my hands in the air. "Easy, boys," I say in my mother tongue.

My father sits in the shadows in the chair by the window.

"Papa."

He signals to his men, and two of them push past me into the hallway to inspect it.

"Where is he?"

"Oh, see that's the thing." I toss my hair and stride in like I'm the queen of the castle. "There is no *he.*"

My father's eyes narrow. "What are you talking about?"

"I needed to know for myself if it was true."

"What are these riddles?" he snaps.

"You sex traffic women. I found out all about it." None of this is a lie, and I let my disgust and bitterness show as fury, even though I'm trembling with fear. This isn't my usual demeanor with my father. I can be petulant and bratty, but that still came from a lack of power.

This is the first time I've met my dad as an equal. A woman, not a child. For the first time, I'm not afraid of losing his love—a love I probably never had in the first place.

"I wanted you to see how it felt to believe your own daughter was being abused the way those women are."

My father surges to his feet, and it takes everything in me not to flinch. The truth is, as much as I desperately wanted this man to love me, as much as I sulked and bratted and played the opposite role of good little girl, underneath it all, I'm terrified of him.

I've seen him kill a man right in front of me. Not recently—it was years ago when I was quite young—one of his men angered him, and he slit his throat in our living room. My mom had grabbed me and locked the two of us in a bathroom until my father apologized and promised he'd never let his wife or daughter see violence in their home again. I think I compartmentalized that incident because I didn't know how to reconcile it with the man I needed in my life to survive.

But I don't need him anymore. I honestly don't want him anymore. If Adrian had taken the time to ask me what I wanted, I could have told him that. If he thinks sparing my father was a gift to me, he's wrong.

He stalks to me now and fists my new coat to shake me. "What are you saying?" he shouts.

I beam up at him like I'm proud. "I kidnapped myself," I tell him.

He releases the jacket and backhands me. I hit the floor, pain exploding in my cheek. I'm both shocked and unsurprised. He's never hit me before, but I certainly knew he was capable of it.

Determined not to break, I cling to my indignation and scramble up to my feet. "How did it feel?" I demand.

"Leave us," my father commands his men. "Go to the hangar." They file out of the room, shutting the door behind them.

I can't decide if it's better or worse to be alone with him.

He slaps me again, this time with an open hand, and I realize my old life has finally and completely crumbled. I can never go back to being that needy unloved girl who was acting out to get her father's attention. This is it. I'm all grown up.

And I have no idea how I will come out of this.

14

Adrian

Sleep feels impossible tonight, so I pace the hotel room some more before I think to call Nadia and let her know I'm on my way.

"Hi Adrian," she says in English. Good—she's practicing the language. That will be a huge step in her feeling more comfortable in Chicago.

"Hey. How are you?"

"Everything's fine here. How about you?"

"I'm heading back tomorrow."

"So…what happened? Did you…finish it?"

I sit on the bed and rest my elbows on my knees. "Ah… no. No, I didn't, Nadia." I clear my throat. "I'm going to let it go." Guilt and shame crowd me from both directions.

"What happened, Adrian?"

"No, nothing happened. Everything's okay."

"Adrian, can you do something for me?"

I swallow down the lump in my throat. "Yeah, anything."

"Stop lying. I know something happened, and I know

something's wrong. I'm not so fragile that you have to protect me. I deserve to know what's going on."

My heart thuds painfully against my sternum. "Yeah. You're right. Okay…" I take a deep breath and let it out, stabbing my fingers through my hair. "I had a lead on Leon Poval. He has a daughter who is about the same age as you living in England."

Nadia sucks in a shocked breath but says nothing.

"I, um, I kidnapped her."

"What? Adrian! Oh my God, you are out of your mind! How could you do–"

"I didn't hurt her, Nadia. I mean, I only planned to make Poval think she was in danger, so he'd come and rescue her, but, ah…"

"You came to your senses."

A whisper of relief hits me at her understanding. "Yes. Exactly."

"Where is she?" Nadia asks. "Is she with you?"

Fresh pain seeps in at me from all sides. "No. I returned her to her father."

"Is she safe with him?"

A cold slithery snake moves through my stomach. *Is she?*

She's his daughter, so of course she is. Yet memories of all the things she said about him creep back in, especially the last one–where she broke down with the realization that he'd probably killed her mother.

Is she safe with him?

The question rattles around in my head, and with every second that passes, awareness creeps over me. What if I left her in the lion's den? I thought I was doing her a favor, I thought I was returning her to safety. But ultimately, she's not safe with that man. Not emotionally. And maybe not even physically. After all, she suspects he killed her mother.

Maybe I didn't do her any favors by letting him go free.

"I don't know," I manage to say to Nadia. My voice sounds choked. "Fuck, I hope so."

"You care about this woman, don't you?"

I don't know how Nadia was able to read that into my words. But I admit it. "Yes."

And because it's Nadia, who's shown so much vulnerability in the last year just telling her stories, I'm willing to say to her what I barely have admitted to myself. "I think I fell in love."

"You think, or you know?"

"I love her, Nadia. And I fucked it up."

"Adrian, you need to go back and fight for her," Nadia says with total clarity. In fact, she sounds stronger and more sure of herself than I've heard her in years. Like this is the one thing she knows about. I'm inclined to believe her. I sure as hell know that trusting my own plan hasn't turned out well.

"Yeah. I should...I should just make sure."

"Make it right, Adrian."

"I thought I was," I lament as I shove my feet back in my boots. "But it feels all wrong."

"You'll figure it out. Don't come home until you're sure, okay? I'm doing fine here. I have a routine and ...friends."

My chest tightens. It's the first time she's called the people in our building friends, and I'm so grateful she feels that way.

"Okay, I'll call you later."

"Tell her you love her," Nadia calls out as I'm hanging up.

I don't know if she wants that. But I do need to know

she's okay. I put a location tracking app on her phone before I gave it back. I pull it up now. She's back at the Radisson. Maybe I'll head over there–just to see that everything's fine. I'm sure it is. Poval's her father, after all. He wouldn't hurt her. Why would he?

Yet, something has me running down the stairs instead of using the elevator. I'm already calling up a ride share app on my phone, but when I get outside, I find a taxi dropping someone off from the airport, and I jump in.

"Take me to the Radisson Blu Astrid," I tell him.

The taxi driver grunts in acknowledgement and moves swiftly through the quiet, dark streets. I jump out at the hotel. The doorman recognizes me and holds open the door.

Inside, I take the elevator up, knowing how stupid this is. If I'm seen here by Poval or any of his men, they will kill me. I don't even have a weapon–I dropped the gun in a garbage can on my way to the airport because I knew I couldn't get it through security.

And yet I can't turn back.

Every time I think of Kat, panic rises up in my throat.

I step off the elevator, all my senses alert. No one is in the hallway. I creep toward the room. There's probably no one here. Maybe they've left the country already. Poval probably has a private plane.

And then I hear a cry of pain from our room, and I rush forward.

Kat!

I still have the keycard to the room since I never checked out, and I yank it out of my back pocket now and hold it to the keylock.

The pad flashes a green light, and I throw the door open wide. Kat's on her knees, her face bruised and bloody. Her father has her by her hair.

His focus jerks to mine.

I have surprise on my side, and I use it, rushing at and tackling Poval to the ground. He shouts something in his native tongue. I bludgeon his face with my fist, breaking his nose, knocking in teeth.

I hear Kat's voice, and it fuels my fury. I can't make out what she's saying, only know that he fucking hurt her. He deserves to die.

He fights me, but he's short, older and has a big paunchy gut. He's clearly out of shape.

"You like to hurt women?" I hiss.

"He has a gun!" Kat cries out. I battle him for it, slamming his wrist back against the floor until it shakes free.

She picks it up and points it at his head.

Poval barks something at Kat in Ukrainian, and her lip lifts in a sneer.

"*Where's. My. Mother?*" I don't even recognize her voice—it carries so much venom. Gone is the wild, rambunctious girl I met a few short days ago. The one who couldn't be dented by me or anyone else in her path.

This one is owning her pain. Embracing it. And using it to fuel a firestorm.

I dig in my pocket for a stray zip tie while she delivers a kick to Poval's ribs.

"I asked you a question, old man. Where is she?"

He spits out blood and gives her a nasty grin. "In her grave."

Kat tries to shoot but the safety is on. Poval flinches, seemingly shocked that she actually wanted him dead.

"*Don't.* Don't, *malyshka.*" I flip Poval to his belly and yank his wrists behind him to zip tie them together. "You don't have to. Interpol wants him. He won't walk free."

I zip tie his ankles, then drag him toward the bed and attach his wrists to the frame of the bed.

Kat doesn't lower the pistol. She keeps it aimed at Poval in trembling hands, her eyes bright with unshed tears, her mouth set in a grim line.

"Give me the gun, sweetheart. Please." I stand and hold my hand out.

She doesn't look away from her father.

"We'll go. You and I. Together, if you'll have me. Give me the gun, and we can walk away. You shoot him and things get complicated. Please, *malyshka*. Let me have it."

She remains indecisive for another moment, but when I slowly move to take it from her, she lets go and falls into my arms.

"That's it, Kit-Kat. You're free of him now. We both are free. We have each other."

She turns her face up to me, and when I see the blooming bruise on her cheekbone and swollen lip, I almost regret my decision not to let her kill him.

Except I don't want her to live with that, nor can I ask her to live with me if I'm the one who shoots him.

Worse than all the bruises is the hurt shining in her eyes. "You left me," she says through trembling lips.

"Mistake," I blurt, so incredibly relieved to have her in my arms again. "Big fucking mistake. I was stupid. I never should have walked away."

She tries to rest her cheek against my chest, then winces and changes sides.

Her father spits some kind of vitriol our way, but I can't understand him.

Kat's body shakes against mine. I keep an arm around her as I text the Interpol number Ravil sent me with the hotel and room number and a photo of Leon Poval.

"Let's get out of here." I tuck the gun in my waistband at my back and retrieve my jacket from the shopping bag on its side by the door. I take her hand to lead her out of the room.

"His men are at the hangar," she says when we shut the door behind us.

"I'll tell Interpol." I send another text to the number with that information. "I'd rather leave before they get here, though." I lead her to the elevator, and once we're inside, I gather her against me again.

"Why was he hurting you, Kat?"

She lifts her chin. "I told him I kidnapped myself."

"Kat," I breathe in dismay. "You shouldn't have."

Her lips tremble again. "Did you really think I'd give him your name?"

I smooth her hair down where Poval mussed it. "No," I say softly. "But I would not have blamed you if you had."

"I could forgive everything, Adrian," she says, eyes tear-bright again, "except you leaving me."

My heart lurches and trips then races ahead.

"Never again," I swear.

"You were supposed to keep me."

"I *am* keeping you," I say immediately. "I'm taking you to Chicago with me. You'll have your clay studio where you can teach me how to center."

"Adrian." She sounds broken.

"I'm sorry, Kateryna. I wanted to make things right, but I fucked that up, too."

"You're keeping me?" She's doing a sulky-weepy thing that soaks me with love.

I scoop her into my arms as the elevator doors open. "Yes. Forever. Are you keeping me?" I stride out.

She tucks her face against my neck, her slender arms looping over my shoulders. "I don't do the keeping. I'm kept."

"Right, of course," I soothe. "Will you be kept by me?"

The doorman holds the door open for me and smiles, not seeing Kat's bruises.

"Can I call you *Daddy?*"

"No."

"Master?"

I make a sound of distaste.

"Why not?"

The sound of sirens approaching the building hastens my steps toward a taxi in front.

"Maybe Master," I concede as I lower her to the ground and open the back door to the cab. "We'll see."

She claps her hands together with glee. Her tears have already dried up. "You do it so well."

I give the driver the name of my hotel and tuck her into my side. "I have asshole down to a T."

"Wouldn't that be an A?" I love that she's getting cute. It's a sign she's feeling more like herself. "You're not an asshole. Okay, sometimes you are, but I like it."

"I know you do," I murmur against her temple. "And I like giving you what you like."

She tips her face up to me and flutters her lashes. "How do you get me so well?"

I shrug. "I don't know. Maybe because I'm close with my sister."

Kat gasps in excitement. "I get to meet Nadia! Oh no– do you think she'll hate me?"

"No. She told me not to come back until I'd made things right with you."

"She did?" I love Kat's expression of awe.

"*Da.* She somehow guessed that I was madly in love with you and gave it to me straight."

Kat's face crumples, and she's suddenly sobbing.

"*Malyshka.* Baby. *Gospodi*, what is it?" I pull her onto my lap and press my lips to her hair.

"Are you? Madly in love with me? Really?" Her wet face nuzzles into my neck.

"Really and truly. Madly, Kit-Kat."

She sniffs. "But you barely know me. What if we get to Chicago and you change your mind?"

I scoff. "I know you. I *know you,* Kat. I may not know all the details, but I know the essence. I know you possess all the qualities I don't. You're bright and happy and resilient. You remain cheerful in the face of great adversity. You attach quickly and forgive easily. You're playful and kind and kinky as fuck." I lower my voice on the last part, so the cab driver won't hear.

She gives a watery laugh. "Are you really in love, or do you just feel responsible for me? Because I know you, too, Adrian. You function from guilt."

My stomach jumps a little with the heave of that very emotion. "I do feel guilty, yes." I massage the back of her neck with my fingers. "But I want something from you, Kat. More than forgiveness."

"What do you want?" she whispers.

"You," I murmur back. "I want you. I want you underneath me, making those enthusiastic sounds before you come." My lips are against her ear, so the words are for her alone. "I want you on your knees with that pouty little mouth around my cock. I want you over my lap getting your pretty ass turned pink."

She squirms on my lap, her belly shaking with soft laughter.

"But it's not just sex. I want you, Kit-Kat. I want–fuck, I *need*–to be your center. The axis you spin around. The place where there is no wobble."

"Adrian," she whispers.

"I want to be around when you're filling up every room with your big personality."

184

"Are you calling me *extra?*" she demands with mock offense.

"You are definitely extra."

She holds my gaze. "What happens when you change your mind?"

My sweet Kateryna—so wounded by her father's abandonment. I will teach her to rely on me. I'll be her rock. "I won't change my mind. Nothing you do or say will ever make me leave. You know why, *malyshka?*" I take on a teasing tone.

"Why?"

The corners of my lips tug upward. "Because I know how to handle you when you misbehave."

Her thighs squeeze together, and she wiggles again.

"I'm going to take good care of you, Kat. I promise."

"I'm going to take good care of you, too." She turns on her sex kitten eyes, and now I'm the one who needs to readjust in his seat.

The cab pulls up in front of my hotel, and we get out. "Wanna go start?" I ask, taking her hand.

"Start what?"

"Taking good care of each other."

She smiles back at me with that easy trust. "I think we've already been doing that."

15

Kat

"Okay, so it's Ravil, Lucy, and their baby, Benjamin, and then Maxim and Sasha, and Oleg and Story on the top floor."

Adrian nods. We're driving from the airport after taking a first-class flight to Chicago. I used my money to buy the tickets because I now have the five million dollars Adrian extorted out of my father.

I plan to give it to Nadia to compensate for the horrors my dad inflicted on her, but it was nice to use my debit card for a posh flight and pull a stack of cash out of the ATM.

We had to wait two days in Adrian's hotel for one of his bratva brothers in England to break into my apartment and get my passport, so I wouldn't have to ride to Chicago on a freight ship. They were also kind enough to pack all my personal belongings and ship them to America.

Adrian asked if I wanted him to fly back there with me, so we could do it ourselves, but I didn't. I'm ready to just shut the door on my old life.

My past means nothing. My father is dead to me. I had no real friends in Liverpool. I will miss the pottery studio, but Adrian promises there will be wheels and classes in Chicago. It's a big city.

"Sasha has a big personality, too, so you two will either love or hate each other," Adrian tells me.

My belly lurches. "You don't think she'll like me?"

Adrian's lips tug. "I didn't say that. She's a lot like you—she likes everyone. But she's also an actor, and she loves to be the center of attention."

I pout. "I don't have to be the center of attention."

Adrian's relaxed in his seat—more relaxed than I've seen him, sending me amused glances as I work out my nervous energy. "Let me ask you this, *malyshka*—are you going to be prancing around the Kremlin in school-girl outfits?"

The Kremlin, I've learned, is the nickname for his building because it mostly houses Russians and Russian-owned businesses.

"How else will I signal that I'm feeling naughty?"

Adrian's smile is indulgent. "You know that means a lot of guys are going to get punched out by me, right?"

"What do you mean?"

"I mean, they're going to look at you, and it's going to piss me off, so I'm going to have to bash heads in."

I laugh, delighted by his future jealousy. "Maybe I'll just wear the outfits for you, then," I tell him.

His eyes glitter with appreciation. "Would you do that for me?"

"If you told me to." I twirl the end of one of my braids. "It could be a rule."

Adrian shifts to adjust himself, and my nipples tighten knowing he's turned on. "It's a rule," he says gruffly.

He hasn't been forceful with me in the way I love in the past two days. I think the bruises on my face disturb him

187

too much. Most of the time before we flew to America was spent with him holding ice packs to my cheek and making sure my every need was taken care of. It was damn sweet. Even the sex was sweet, which was nice, but not necessarily my thing.

Fortunately, Adrian still seems quite willing to play my game.

"I was wrong," he says, "you're not like Sasha. She has an exhibitionist streak. You...well, you've got a thing for authority. No?"

"Just yours."

He makes an approving sound. "You say all the right things."

"So, Maykl is the doorman and your friend from Russia, and Nikolai is the hacker."

"No, Dima is the hacker—Nikolai's twin. Nikolai is the bookie."

"And which one has the Russian girlfriend?"

"That's Dima."

"And Story is the rock star."

"Right."

I've been quizzing him non-stop about his life in Chicago—partly to distract myself from the end of my old life. Partly because I want to know what to expect. I want to fit in and make friends and say the right things.

"What about your *pakhan*? Will he hate me because of my father?"

Adrian reaches for my hand and laces his fingers through mine. "Definitely not. He's not a hater. He keeps a cool head about everything. Very strategic—not much drama." I open my mouth to start a line of questioning about Lucy, but Adrian says, "Kateryna."

"What?"

"Everyone will love you."

"How do you know?"

"Because that's how they are. And because there's nothing about you not to love. And because I love you."

Tears pop in my eyes. I'm not tired of hearing it yet.

I guess it's three words I haven't heard enough of in my life, and coming from Adrian, they mean everything.

"I want them to like me," I admit.

"I know. And they will."

I catch a glimpse of water right before Adrian turns into an underground parking lot.

"Is this it?" I gasp. "You didn't tell me it's right on the water!"

I don't know what I'd pictured–something very utilitarian. Definitely not fancy.

But then, I probably should have known based on the vehicle we're in. I know American cars are bigger, but this shiny black SUV seems enormous and posh.

He parks, and I hop out, pleased when he gathers my hand to lead me to the elevator. It's such a simple gesture– hand holding–but feels like a claiming.

I'm going to take good care of you, Kat.

I still keep thinking he's going to change his mind any moment, but I liked his reasoning about why he wouldn't.

"Where are we going first? Straight to your apartment? Will Nadia be there?"

"Yes." Adrian pulls me against him. "You don't ever have to be nervous when you're with me. I have your back. Always."

"Okay." I sound breathless. I bounce my knees in the elevator and shimmy. "I just want her to like me. I'm sorry–I'm really nervous," I say.

We get off the elevator, and we pass an old woman in

the hallway. Adrian greets her in Russian, then presents me, "Valentina, this is Kateryna, my girlfriend. She's moving in today."

The older woman reaches for my hand and clasps it. She greets me in Russian, and Adrian says to her, "Kat isn't Russian. She's from Ukraine." To me, he says, "Kat, my sister works with Valentina cleaning and nannying for Ravil."

"It's so nice to meet you," I say, not sure if she understands, but she bobs her head.

"Nice to meet you, too. Welcome to the Kremlin."

"Thank you."

A door opens at the end of the hall, and a young woman steps out. "Adrian!"

"Is that Nadia?" I ask.

Nadia hesitates like there's an invisible forcefield keeping her within the boundaries of the apartment, but then with seeming effort, breeches it and steps out into the hallway.

When I approach, she opens her arms wide. I think she's going to hug Adrian, but it's me she gathers. "Sister," she says in a thick accent.

My eyes water. Are we sisters? God, how I wished for a sibling growing up. I hug her back. "I was afraid you'd hate me," I confess, unable to keep the worry to myself.

Nadia pulls back. Her expression is serious–I get the feeling it's always this somber. "No," she says firmly. "You are my sister." There's a fierceness to her words, and just like that, I feel claimed again.

For once, I belong somewhere. With people who want me. Who know the worst things about me–who my father is and what he's done, as well as my neediness, my attention-craving, my naughtiness–and still claim me as one of their own.

Adrian takes my hand and gently tugs me into his apartment. It's stunning—open and bright with large picture windows overlooking the water. It's new and modern and absolutely beautiful.

"Welcome home," Adrian murmurs.

"Is this real?" I turn into him, blinking back the moisture in my eyes.

He drops his duffel bag and wraps his arms around me. "You're mine now," he assures me. "This is where I'm keeping you. Right here. With me."

I reach for his shoulders and use them to leap up into his arms, straddling his waist like a child. "Promise?"

He nips my breast and carries me toward a bedroom. "Mmm hmm. Let me show you what happens if you try to escape."

I giggle and look back over my shoulder at Nadia, who wears a startled smile.

"I'm going downstairs," Nadia announces loudly.

Adrian stops and turns, like he's surprised. "You are?"

"Yes," she says casually, but I know from what Adrian's told me about her, it's hard for her to get out of the apartment. "The Storytellers are practicing, and I want to listen. Besides, you two need time to settle in."

Adrian hesitates then pushes forward. "Thank you, Nadia." He shuts the door behind us.

"Is that unusual?" I whisper when he pivots and sets me on my feet, standing on the bed. I kick off my boots and jump on it.

He kicks his off, too. "Totally unusual. I...have mixed feelings about it."

I reach for him to pull him up on the bed, too, and he delights me by following me, bouncing on it with me. "Why?"

"I think she has a crush on Flynn, Story's brother, and he's a player. I don't like it."

I give a scandalized gasp because I love every part of this convo–knowing the ins and outs about Adrian's family, hearing about secret crushes, loving that this Flynn is getting Nadia out of the apartment.

"I think it's good. If it makes her feel normal again, it can't be a bad thing."

"And when he hurts her?" Adrian demands.

"Maybe she'll do the hurting," I say with a shrug. "You never know." I stop bouncing and loop my arms around his neck. "I like your bed," I murmur.

"I like having you in my bed," he replies. "Now…" –he raises a stern brow– "*Strip*."

The muscles between my legs catch and release, and I scramble to obey. I tear off the clothes he bought me in Antwerp, then drop to my knees and unbuckle his belt. "Did I say you could suck my cock, *malyshka*?"

I freeze, looking up at him, my heart hammering with excitement.

"That comes after your spanking."

My internal muscles flutter again. "Okay, Daddy."

His lips twitch, but he shakes his head. "It's Master."

I shimmy with excitement. "Okay, Master."

He toys with my breast for a moment, just gazing down at me, then lifts his chin. "On your forearms and knees. Let me see that pretty ass presented."

I comply, pushing my ass up for him.

He lowers to kneel behind me and strokes his palm over my cheeks a few times before he delivers the first spank. It's firm and stingy and makes me wiggle my butt for more.

He starts slowly, alternating right and left cheek, then gradually picks up speed.

I moan and pant, my arousal leaking between my legs the more the burn increases. I'm gasping by the time he stops and rubs his fingers between my legs. I'm wet and swollen for him, totally ready.

"Who do you belong to, Kateryna?"

I smile into the bedcovers. "You, Master."

He delivers several hard spanks–hard enough to make me gasp. "Say my name."

"Adrian. Adrian Turgenev. I belong to Adrian."

"Mmm." He rewards me with stroking around my cheeks then between my legs.

I'm shaking now, about to start begging.

"Who owns this pussy, Kateryna?" He screws one digit inside me.

"You do," I warble.

"Who makes you come?"

"Only you," I gasp, on the cusp of coming right now.

He pushes my knees wider and opens his pants. Thank *God*.

"Are you going to come all over this cock, Kateryna?" He presses the velvety hard head of his cock against my entrance.

I don't know what got into Adrian–where all this dirty talk came from–but I am praising every deity there is right now. I knew he could do dominant, but this is an entirely new level.

"Yes, Master," I gasp.

"I'm going to make you come all night long, *malyshka*." He pushes in and eases back then presses forward again.

"Yes, please."

He grips my hips and pulls my ass back to meet his steady thrusts. "Any time you need a good hard fucking and a reminder of who you belong to, what are you going to do, *printsessa*?"

I gasp at how deep he's getting in me. This is the best angle ever. "Wear my sexy schoolgirl outfit."

"That's right." He keeps plowing into me, owning me, possessing me, breaking me in as his. I love it so much I grow dizzy.

"I need to buy a new one," I remember.

"You'll need lots of them," he rumbles, picking up speed. "One for every day of the week. Because I won't be giving this pussy a break."

I come a little.

Adrian feels the squeezing of my muscles and reaches around to rub my clit and help me with it, going still inside me while I release. "That's one," he murmurs, like there's going to be many more before the night is through. Then he pulls my arms behind my back and pushes my torso flat on the bed to give it to me even harder.

"Are you going to be my little sex doll?"

"Yes, please," I beg, my eyes rolling back in my head.

This guy couldn't do it any better. I love his dirty talk as much as I love his huge heroic heart. His boundless capacity for accepting me as I am. A trait his sister and friends seem to share as well.

"I know you thought sex in Antwerp was boring. I was just letting you rest up. Because now I'm going to use and abuse you for the rest of your life."

I come again. Screw Delaney and resolving my daddy issues. I think they're working out just fine for me. Perfectly, actually. I can't imagine anyone loving vanilla sex as much as I love this.

"That's two, *dietka*. You'd better come again when I tell you, or there will be hell to pay."

"I will," I gasp, aftershocks running through me.

He pulls out, and I moan at the loss, but it's just to tug my legs straight, so I'm flat on my belly. I spread them for him, tilting my ass a little. He reenters, and I moan again in satisfaction. "You like that, *malysh*? You like being filled by me?"

"Yes, Master."

He slams in harder, and I love it–the deep strokes a different angle this time. I reach between my legs and touch my own clit. "Kat...Kit-Kat," he chants, his movements growing jerky. "You're mine now...I won't let you go."

Somehow, he knows to say everything I need to hear.

"Please," I beg, already needing to come again. Already desperate to receive his pleasure as a full completion. A full claiming. A complete actualization of who we are as a new couple.

"*Blyad'*," he curses, his breath holding then gusting out then holding again. "Kat...Kateryna...*yes*!" He shoves in deep, his cock pulsing inside me as he empties his balls.

I shake with sobs of ecstasy, my own muscles seizing around his member, drawing him deeper, milking his finish. "Please," I whimper, even though he's already come. He's already given me everything I crave.

He lowers his body over mine, kissing my nape, biting me, showing me it's not over yet. It's not ever over with us.

I'm dissolving in his arms–floating away as tiny bits of energy into the universe. And yet, I've never felt so collected. So held and absorbed. "Don't let me go," I whimper, not wanting this moment to end. Wanting to keep it forever.

"Never, Kat," he says fiercely. "Not ever, ever."

"I love you," I murmur.

"I'll *always* love you," he answers.

A deep breath of air rushes in–deeper than I knew possible. For the first time in my life, I can breathe.

And Adrian is my oxygen.

My center axis.
My everything.

EPILOGUE

Adrian

Bratva tattoos are given as a ritual. They are used to represent status within the organization. Even though Ravil has dropped or ignored some of the brotherhood's traditions, inking isn't one of them.

Our souls and our skin bear the mark of our crimes. We remember each act and measure it against our contributions to our brothers. Balance in brotherhood. These were the words our *pakhan* spoke after I killed four of Poval's men when I broke into the sofa factory and freed my sister. He spoke them again when I returned to burn the place down. Each crime merits a marking on our skin. Some wear them with pride. Some as penance.

Today I complete the one I bear for kidnapping Kat. I wear it as my penance. So that I never forget her sacrifice and forgiveness that brought us together.

Stepan, our tattoo artist, takes every story into consideration when he creates his art, including our own emotions around the event. The tattoo he gave me for burning down the factory was proud and powerful. This one is more tender. He used knotted rope to depict Kat's captivity. It coils around my shoulder, then snakes around my arm to form a manacle around my wrist—a symbol of the bond we now have. I captured her, but now I'm forever tied to her.

Kat wanted her own markings, which Stepan finished last week. I wouldn't allow her to ink her skin with anything related to her father, but she accepted the symbol of manacles—to show she's been claimed by me—forever owned, kept, and cared for. She wears twin cuffs drawn as rope with a knot in the shape of a heart on the inside of each wrist. A perfect place for me to kiss every time I hold her hand.

Stepan sits back now and nods.

I'm surrounded by the senior members of the bratva—Ravil, Maxim, Oleg, Nikolai, as well my friend Maykl, and several other members. Gleb, a seventy-year-old bratva brother who'd been part of a different cell and recently found his way to us, pours vodka all around.

Ravil clears his throat, and the room falls silent. "Our souls and our skin bear the mark of our crimes. We remember each act and measure it against our contributions to our brothers. Balance in brotherhood." He raises his glass.

"Balance in brotherhood. To our brother." Maxim raises his.

"Balance in brotherhood. To our brother." Each member present takes his turn, lifting his glass and holding my gaze.

"Balance in brotherhood." I lift mine, and we all drink.

The men thump me on the back, and we file out of Stepan's second-floor studio.

"Ready to surprise your girl?" Maxim asks.

I nod. "Ready."

"Sasha says the women are finished prepping." He looks up from a text on his phone. "You go get Kat, and we'll join the women."

I spent the past three and a half weeks moving mountains to put together a clay studio for Kat. It's on the first floor because the kiln will have to be installed in the basement, and I want her to be able to have easy access. Also, Ravil gave her a street-facing window, so she can display her creations, if she ever feels comfortable.

I've been able to keep the entire endeavor a secret, pretending I've been busy with work for Ravil and haven't had a chance to even look into fulfilling my promise to her yet. Sasha–who always loves a party–decided to throw Kat a "surprise studio" party. She, Nadia, Lucy, Story, and Nikolai's girlfriend, Chelle, spent the last hour decorating it with balloons and flowers and are waiting there now to jump out and yell *surprise.*

I take the elevator up with the same giddy satisfaction coursing through my veins I get every time I go to our apartment.

Living with Kat is an intense pleasure. If I hadn't been so determined to honor my offer of building her this studio, I never would have left her side. Despite everything being new and me leaving her alone far too much, Kat remains upbeat. She's been feeling her way into life here, getting close with Nadia, making friends with many of the women in the building, especially Sasha and Story. She found a pottery class and is thinking about enrolling in community college.

We received word that her father will be extradited to Italy to face murder charges there. If he's released, he faces proceedings in two other countries, so the chance of him going free are slim. Kat offered the entirety of the ransom her father paid for her to Nadia who refused. Ultimately, we agreed to split it half and half. Ravil and Maxim helped me set it up into investments, so we can all live comfortably off the dividends. While I'm grateful for the ease it brings all of us, part of me hopes Nadia won't use it as an excuse to stop working. Getting her out of the apartment is crucial for her mental well-being.

I unlock the apartment door and find Kat waiting in—*Lord help me*—a new school girl outfit. This one has a pleated red plaid skirt and with a matching plaid collar around her throat. The white socks are thigh high and the crisp white blouse is open three buttons.

My dick instantly gets rock hard, and I literally groan out loud at the sight of her.

"Nadia disappeared, so I thought we could—" she cuts off into giggles when I throw her over my shoulder and start marching toward the bedroom.

But wait. I stop in my tracks.

"What?"

Ack.

I can't.

Everyone's waiting downstairs.

I pivot then set her back down. "*Malyshka*, you know I'm dying to take you into that bedroom and turn your pretty ass pink."

"But?"

"But I have a surprise for you first." I eye her outfit. I did make the rule that the outfits are only for my eyes, but she looks adorable, and I trust my brothers. Maybe that rule can be modified. I button one of the buttons and pull a piece of cloth out of my pocket. "Turn around and close your eyes."

"Ooh. Are you going to tie me up, too?"

"Mmm, you'd like that, wouldn't you, *dietka*?" I tie the cloth around her head to cover her eyes.

"Yes. As long as it's not with a zip tie. I don't ever want to see a zip tie again in my life."

"I'm not tying you up right now, *malysh*. But I will later–I promise."

"Is this about your tattoo? May I see it?"

"Later. Right now is your surprise." I propel her toward the door.

"Oh! Are we going somewhere?"

"*Da.*" I lead her to the elevator, and we take it down to the first floor.

"Are we driving somewhere?"

"*Nyet.*"

"Are we leaving the building?"

"*Nyet.* No more questions, Kateryna. Just wait."

I lead her to the studio and open the door. Our friends are packed into the space, waiting with the lights off.

"Where are we?"

I untie the blindfold, and someone flips on the lights.

"Surprise!" everyone yells. Confetti flies at us from all directions. The women made the studio festive with streamers and balloons and flowers. A banner reading "Kremlin Clay" has been strung across the back. Ice buckets with champagne perch on silver stands, and a giant charcuterie board is on the table packed with fancy meat, cheese, berries, honeycomb and crackers.

Kat screams and stumbles backward into my arms. She covers her mouth with her hands. "Oh my God. What is this? Oh my God!"

"Welcome to your new studio, Kremlin Clay," I tell her, rocking her slowly as she takes it all in.

"Wh-what?" she says faintly. "This is…mine?"

"That's right, *dietka*. Thanks to Ravil," –I nod at my *pakhan*– "for giving us this space. And to all my brothers who helped me get it ready."

She takes in the studio. I consulted with the teacher at the nearby studio where she started classes to find out everything she would need. The space is roomy, with ceramic tile floors and countertops for easy clean up and two large industrial sinks at the back. There's one wheel, but room for more, in case she ever wants to hold classes here. I built utilitarian shelving units in the back to hold her works in progress and nicer ones in the front to display finished work.

"The kiln will be delivered in a few weeks, but I already have the electrical set up for it. It will go in the basement, which you can get to through those stairs." I point to the door at the rear of the studio. "The windows are frosted for now, but if you ever decide to display your wares, they can be made clear." I point toward the front of the studio that faces the street.

Kat turns to face me. Her skin is blotchy with color. She buries her face against my chest and bursts into tears.

"Aw, I think that means she likes it." Sasha winks at me.

I try to calm the racket of my heart ricocheting against my chest. They are happy tears, but they still make me want to move mountains to see her smile.

"I love it," she sobs against me. "Oh my God, I can't stop crying." She lifts her face and mops her tears. "This was so nice of you." She turns. "All of you. I can't believe you did this for me."

"Of course, we did," Sasha says easily. "You're part of the crew now."

That only makes Kat cry harder. Even my own eyes mist because I know how much this sense of belonging means to her. She hasn't had a family she could rely on before. I'm resolved to give that to her each and every day. To make sure she knows she belongs here. Not just with me but with us.

"Thank you." She tries her best to get a hold of herself.

Nikolai pops a bottle of champagne and hands it to Chelle, who starts pouring in the glasses lined up on the counter.

"Come on, let's toast." Sasha tugs Kat forward and hands her a glass of champagne as Nikolai pops a second cork. "You don't have to make this into a retail location, you could always keep it as your private studio but have monthly open studio nights. You could even invite other artists."

I smile to myself as Sasha brainstorms.

"Absolutely," Chelle agrees. "I'd be happy to help with your publicity, if you did."

"You guys are making me cry again," Kat complains, wiping her tears. She puts her glass down and throws an arm around each of the women. "I love you so much, do you know that?"

"Aw, we love you, too, sweetheart," Sasha says.

"We do," my sister agrees in her soft voice.

When everyone has a glass, Sasha lifts hers. "To Kremlin Clay and her resident artist, Kateryna!"

"To Kateryna," I murmur, clinking my glass to hers. "I love you."

"*Vashe zdorov'ye.*" The Russians in the room all give the Russian toast.

"Cheers," Chelle and Story say with a laugh, clinking their glasses together.

"Thank you, Adrian." Kat's eyes swim with tears again.

I lean my forehead against hers as glasses clink around us. She sets her glass down, and I catch her two wrists and trace my thumbs over her pulse points, where the tattooed knots lie. "You're mine," I murmur.

"Say it again."

"You're mine. Forever, *malyshka*."

She traces the pathway of my new tattoo down my arm to my wrist then picks up my hand and kisses my pulse. "And this means you're mine."

"Yes. Also forever."

She surges against me, throwing her arms around my neck and pressing her lips to mine. "We're going to have so much fun," she says, and I laugh, pulling her against my body and giving her another kiss. "Yes. Yes, we are."

FOR A SPECIAL **Bonus Epilogue** with Kat, Adrian and Nadia, join Renee's newsletter. If you enjoyed this book, please consider leaving a review. They make an enormous difference for indie authors.

Be sure to read the next book in the series, *The Player*

WANT MORE? THE PLAYER

The Player
(Flynn and Nadia)

Players will play.

Flynn Taylor, rock 'n roll heartthrob, plays fast and loose.

He's with different girls every night. Yes, *girls* plural.

On the brink of becoming not just a Chicago sensation, but an American icon,

he's everything I should avoid.

Then again, maybe it doesn't matter.

I'm so damaged, I'm not even capable of a relationship.

He might be the perfect antidote.

The temptation I need to lure me back to the side of the living.

He could help me get over my trauma. Attempt physical intimacy.

If it goes wrong—no harm, no foul, right?

If only I can keep my overprotective bratva brother from threatening
    to kill him if he even touches me…

Order now

WANT FREE RENEE ROSE BOOKS?

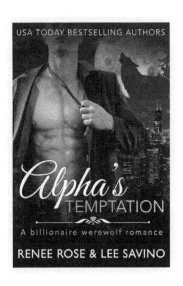

Go to http://subscribepage.com/alphastemp to sign up for Renee Rose's newsletter and receive a free copy of *Alpha's Temptation, Theirs to Protect, Owned by the Marine, Theirs to Punish, The Alpha's Punishment, Disobedience at the*

Dressmaker's and *Her Billionaire Boss*. In addition to the free stories, you will also get special pricing, exclusive previews and news of new releases.

OTHER TITLES BY RENEE ROSE

Chicago Bratva

Vegas Underground Mafia Romance

Contemporary
Daddy Rules Series

Hollywood Daddy

Stepbrother Daddy

Master Me Series

Her Royal Master

Her Russian Master

Her Marine Master

Yes, Doctor

Double Doms Series

Theirs to Punish

Theirs to Protect

Holiday Feel-Good

Scoring with Santa

Saved

Other Contemporary

Black Light: Valentine Roulette

Black Light: Roulette Redux

Black Light: Celebrity Roulette

Black Light: Roulette War

Black Light: Roulette Rematch

Punishing Portia (written as Darling Adams)

The Professor's Girl

Safe in his Arms

Paranormal

Two Marks Series

His Mate and Master

Zandian Pet

Their Zandian Mate

His Human Possession

Zandian Brides

Night of the Zandians

Bought by the Zandians

Mastered by the Zandians

Zandian Lights

Kept by the Zandian

Claimed by the Zandian

Stolen by the Zandian

Other Sci-Fi

The Hand of Vengeance

Her Alien Masters

ABOUT RENEE ROSE

USA TODAY BESTSELLING AUTHOR RENEE ROSE loves a dominant, dirty-talking alpha hero! She's sold over a million copies of steamy romance with varying levels of kink. Her books have been featured in USA Today's *Happily Ever After* and *Popsugar*. Named Eroticon USA's Next Top Erotic Author in 2013, she has also won *Spunky and Sassy's* Favorite Sci-Fi and Anthology author, *The Romance Reviews* Best Historical Romance, and *has* hit the *USA Today* list ten times with her Bad Boy Alpha and Wolf Ranch series, as well as various anthologies.

Please follow her on Tiktok

Renee loves to connect with readers!
www.reneeroseromance.com
reneeroseauthor@gmail.com

facebook.com/reneeroseromance

twitter.com/reneeroseauthor

instagram.com/reneeroseromance

amazon.com/Renee-Rose/e/B008AS0FT0

bookbub.com/authors/renee-rose

Made in the USA
Monee, IL
21 April 2022

95140325R00125